An Imperfect Arrangement

AN IMPERFECT ARRANGEMENT

A Novel

Chris Amisano

iUniverse, Inc.

New York Lincoln Shanghai

An Imperfect Arrangement

iUniverse books may be ordered through booksellers or by contacting:

iUniverse
2021 Pine Lake Road, Suite 100
Lincoln, NE 68512
www.iuniverse.com
1-800-Authors (1-800-288-4677)

Because of the dynamic nature of the Internet, any Web addresses or links contained in this book may have changed since publication and may no longer be valid.

This is a work of fiction. All of the characters, names, incidents, organizations, and dialogue in this novel are either the products of the author's imagination or are used fictitiously.

ISBN: 978-0-595-44125-9 (pbk)
ISBN: 978-0-595-68495-3 (cloth)
ISBN: 978-0-595-88449-0 (ebk)

Printed in the United States of America

In Memory of Artur Cavalier

CHAPTER 1

▼

DISPOSABLE BOY AND THE BITCH

"Yeah, that's right," I mumbled under my breath at the stoplight. "Go on and look. I'm thirty-five, I have a thirty inch-waist, a butt like steel, *and* a BMW to put them in."

The grungy twenty-something guy in the Jeep next to me stared with curious interest after trying hard to start a race.

"Old enough to be your father," I said out loud.

The light turned green and I floored the car, leaving him in a cloud of dust and testosterone. I would be alone for at least another hour when I got home, so I hurried to beat the growing afternoon traffic, buzzing in and out past the old oak, elm, and maple trees of midtown Memphis. The antebellum houses, subtly changed with modern renovation, looked down on me in between the trees and the Spanish Moss as they had most of my life, mixing Old South style with New South residents, gay couples sitting happily in one hundred and fifty year old front parlors just as the stiff gentry had done years before. I pulled into the parking lot of my 1920's red brick apartment building and noticed a car and a driver I had definitely not seen before. I had become afraid of missing something if I didn't look around, so the presence of a new guy rarely escaped my notice.

Since my partner Ayers died three years earlier, my ever-present practicality told me that there was no use looking for someone else but every once in a while an almost foreign voice would pipe up to sweet talk me into believing that another romantic opportunity could be lurking behind every one of those old oak trees. The guy smoothly got out of the car, a silver Audi A6. He wore a fitted suit that had obviously been custom tailored and carried the latest Gucci briefcase, as if he had just strutted down the catwalk in the summer 2006 fashion show. He was good looking, with great hair and a perfect bubble butt, the kind that you want to walk up behind and smack. He walked confidently to the staircase leading to the two-bedroom units in the building and nodded to me as I drove past. I lifted a half-hearted wave to make it appear as though I wasn't watching. As I did a normal Alex Palini "I saw you" double-take, he turned to look again in the shadow of the wrought iron staircase, watching me get out of the car, hoist my gym bag over one shoulder and my suit over the other. I made my way to my third floor one-bedroom apartment being watched the entire time, and somehow enjoying it.

I threw everything on the bed and began to take off my wet gym clothes, pausing briefly to criticize myself in the full-length mirror behind the bedroom door. I resisted the temptation to say, "I love you" to the reflection as one of my shrinks had recommended a few years earlier. I grabbed a towel from the linen closet, went into the bathroom, and turned on the shower to let it run for a few seconds. I began to relax as soon as the hot water touched my skin, savoring a few moments of silence.

Suddenly, the shower curtain opened. I was startled, but not really startled; the kind of surprise that is expected but just not timed correctly.

"Stephen," I gasped through the steam. "I wasn't expecting you so soon."

He was already naked and ready to jump into the shower with me. The guy could get out of his clothes quicker than any Friday night velcro stripper.

"Dude, I've heard that older men fantasize about soapy showers with young guys," he said to me as we stood wet and face to face.

I stared at Stephen Clark, my twenty-two year old boyfriend, known to my friends secretly as "Disposable Boy", a former Ole Miss running-back who secretly had sex with his fraternity brothers, a real-life porno flick. I made my usual gesture, a quick nod of my head, giving him permission to get in the shower with me before I could take time to think about it. At times like these, I always went back to the way things started with him.

The day I met Stephen at the gym, I was feeling very good about myself, drying off mock-provocatively in front of my locker. Stephen stepped out of the shower and walked over to his locker, nearly next door to mine. This blonde boy with blue eyes, strong cheekbones, and a very visible attitude captivated me right away. I was also drawn to his midsection, not because of some middle aged horny fantasy but because he was accentuated by a large penis piercing, a silver ring and stud that was at least an inch and a half in diameter. To my eyes any piercing down there looked really big.

My gaydar immediately blipped off the map, and since Ayers was gone, I would have to give in to my need for real intimacy sooner or later. As I dressed, I spoke quickly and cynically to Stephen, who remained naked for some time, purposefully parading himself around the locker room like a gay peacock.

"That must've hurt," I said, nodding toward Stephen's bejeweled member.

"It did, man, but the pleasure from this cancels out the pain of having it done. It's pretty hot for the person who's on the other end, too," Stephen said in a sly voice, pulling up his Calvin Klein boxer briefs with a snap.

I was dressed by this time and had taken several good looks at him. Aside from the piercing, he had a muscular body, the lean curves of someone who probably did not have to worry about what he ate, his hips sitting invitingly on either side of a perfectly smooth, tapered torso. I nodded to him and walked out of the locker room, suddenly becoming shy as I usually did after a few bits of conversation with a hot guy. As I got into my car, Stephen breathlessly ran up to the window and said, "Would you consider telling me your name and having dinner with me sometime?"

I was taken totally by surprise and very unusually stumbled over my words. "God, that's forward. Let's just say my name is Alex and I have plans for dinner, but I can meet you for a drink at Christina's at nine tonight. Will that work?"

I was surprised at how quickly I arranged this meeting, my confidence coming back only after he made the first truly bold move. Maybe after three years I was ready, at the very least, to attempt to have a conversation and a possible connection with a guy before having sex with him. The smile that crossed Stephen's face at that point took my breath away as he answered.

"Cool. I'm Stephen. I can't wait to see how you clean up."

That night, one drink multiplied into a blur. I felt something for him when he explained that one of his fraternity brothers had broken his heart and that he now preferred "more mature" guys. I was also very attracted to the idea that this totally hot frat boy was interested in me.

I came back to the present with a start, finding Stephen on his knees in the shower. I sighed loudly in resignation and desperation because he knew I had a hard time resisting him. When he finished, he stood up and let me move into the spray from the shower. He washed my back, then moved down to my legs, giving the alleged butt of steel a quick peck on his way down. Stephen wasn't the best companion in the world, but he was well trained, like a puppy. Maybe that's why it was so easy to do.

When I finished showering, I quickly kissed Stephen on the lips and stepped out, leaving my young buck to finish alone. Walking into the bedroom, I noticed where he had thrown the contents of his snappy Jack Spade messenger bag onto the dresser. I regarded the small bag of pot with amusement but rolled my eyes at the vials of cocaine lying among the keys and ATM receipts. Somehow I had never seen myself with someone who actually did coke and was this messy about it, but he also knew not to do it around me. Dating Disposable Boy was better than a random online hookup or having a relationship with my right hand, so I believed in my ability to tolerate his flaws without too much of a fuss. Each morning I woke up next to him, there was always a split second where that foreign voice reminded me of the romantic possibilities, but then the practicality took over again to remind me of the microscopic chance I would have at finding someone who could make me as happy as Ayers had. I threw myself onto the bed in the diminishing light of the evening and thought about him, wondering what he would say about Disposable Boy. Would he agree with my self-imposed sentence, the one that made me unable to connect with anyone, or would he tell me that a hot guy right then was better than no guy at all? Then it came to me as it always did, Ayers snapping his fingers in a queeny attempt to make me laugh, while raising his voice a few octaves to shout, "You go, boy!"

CHAPTER 2

▼

NEVER LET THEM SEE
YOU CRY

I woke up in the dark, not sure what had brought me out of my exhausted sleep. Then I heard it, the sound of someone knocking on the back door. I jumped up, slipped on my most comfortable but obviously worn flannel boxers, and flipped on the light. The pot was still on the dresser, but the coke and Stephen's keys were gone. In their place was a note:

Sexy dude-

I'm going to my mothers house—I'll see you later. I hope we're still going out-it is Friday, isn't it? I was pretty good in the shower, wasn't I? Don't do anything nasty 'til I get back.

Stevie

I regarded the note with some disdain because he obviously thought that I sat around and played with myself, waiting for his return.

"See if I leave the bathroom door unlocked again," I said, talking to myself as usual.

I realized again that someone was waiting at the back door. I stumbled through the hallway and made it to the door, pulling the blinds open far enough to reveal the new stranger, the model-like guy with the Audi. Audi man was much more attractive through the kitchen window than he had been from a distance. I guessed he was about six feet tall and he had piercing green eyes and thick dark hair, which was perfectly in order. His expression was so serene, like knocking on a new neighbor's door was no big deal. Aside from their green color, his eyes gave off the same serenity that his face did. His eyelashes were naturally long and seemed to sweep down in slow motion as he blinked beneath his well-manicured eyebrows. He wore running shorts and a tight tank top, revealing a smooth, muscular body, so Audi man appeared to be the perfect package of physical attraction and confidence that we all wanted. I unlocked the door and remembered that I was wearing a pair of boxers and nothing else. He very obviously looked me up and down and then smiled.

"I'm sorry," he spoke with a deep-South accent. "I hope I'm not interruptin' anything ..."

"No, I've been asleep for a while and it's about time I was getting up. Have we met?" I inquired stupidly.

He was still staring at me while he spoke. "No, but I was wondering if you knew how to get in touch with maintenance. There's a leak in my bathroom and it's gotten much worse today. I hope my upstairs neighbor doesn't end up in my tub."

"I wouldn't mind ending up in your tub," I replied innocently.

"Um," he stammered, "are you going to put something on or what?"

"I have the number for maintenance, but before I let you in I would appreciate it if you would introduce yourself," I said, grinning coyly. "I mean, you've practically seen me naked and I don't know your name and I also used my out loud voice a minute ago and I am really embarrassed."

I had just uttered a full sentence in Alex run-on, the name I had given to my nervous language, the one that crept out when I was having a difficult conversation or trying to talk on a first date.

Audi man was almost certainly another gay guy in the gay ghetto, because if a single man moved to midtown Memphis, especially a man who could appear that he had been jogging or to the gym with no visible hairdo damage, there was a high probability that he was gay. Gay men in this neighborhood picked up on each other's gayness like animals on the scent, making friendships, unions, and one-night stands with the greatest of ease and much less grunting.

"I'm Rick Monette," said Audi man, "I've just moved up here from Atlanta. You were the only friendly person I'd seen, if you know what I mean. I just didn't know that I'd get a floor show with it."

I blushed slightly and held out my hand. "I'm Alex Palini, lifetime resident. Come in. You can call maintenance from here. I hope you were out jogging and wanted to get a nice hot soak, because if you dress like that all the time we may have a problem."

As Rick began to reply, the phone rang. I excused myself and reached to pick up the cordless. The voice on the other end was Stephen.

"Dude," he said, "I'm not gonna be coming over there. Mom's sick again. I'm gonna stay here to make sure she doesn't need anything."

More than anything else, I hated being called dude, but the part about Stephen's mom was true. She was still going through heavy chemotherapy, and although things were looking better, she became very sick after her treatments. It was also a good bet that when Stephen's mother finally fell asleep, he would call his brother to share a few lines. The vials of coke that were on my dresser earlier in the afternoon were probably gone already, too. Stephen's growing dependency was springing from the fact that he really couldn't deal with his mother's illness. It made him realize that even at his young age, he was just as mortal as the next person, something that, luckily or unluckily, had hit me full tilt boogie already.

"Allrighty then," I said, "I guess I'll just have to go ahead and do something nasty."

As I said this, an amused grin crossed Rick's face. I looked at him and winked, wondering where I was getting all of this sudden flirtatious ability. Most of my recent attempts at flirtation tended to fall flat, leaving me looking like a miserably humorless dork with a really bad case of low self-esteem.

I wanted to finish my conversation with Disposable Boy and get back to Rick as quickly as possible, so I ended the chat with a half-assed "call me in the morning". I hung up the phone and grabbed my quick-reference pad of necessary phone numbers: pizza delivery, Mandy's Deli, and the apartment office. Turning toward Rick, who I estimated to be a little older than me, I handed him the pad and indicated that maintenance was the first phone number. As he dialed, I tried to make small talk.

"My boy toy cancelled on me," I said, trying to make it sound like a joke.

As Rick waited for someone to help him, I watched him and became aware of the fact that this perfect specimen standing in my kitchen reminded me a little of Ayers: the attitude, the look, the body, the hair, and especially the eyes. As Rick reported his problem, I let my mind wander back to the night I met Ayers.

It had been one of those wild club nights; my friends and I were dancing and drinking, and the air was heavy with cologne, sweat, and smoke, with a dance floor full of shirtless and wildly undulating guys, responsible businessmen during the day and go-go dancer wannabes by night. I saw Ayers dancing on a platform and was struck by his green eyes and totally unconcerned look. I did a patented stare down long enough to show my interest, then we lost sight of each other. Later, a friend of mine brought the smiling Ayers over to meet me. Apparently my friend and Ayers knew each other.

My friend, who was not big on fancy intros, introduced us: "Alex, Ayers. Ayers, Alex."

I reached out my hand and said, "Hi, how are you?"

Ayers looked down and quietly said, "Embarrassed."

Meeting my first real match was a scary thing when it actually happened, especially since I was not familiar with the way my soul reacted at the time. The moment Ayers looked at me that first time, I felt a sensation deep down inside, an emotional version of my foot falling asleep, a tingling that pricked at my insides for a few brief seconds before going away, a loud indication that what had just happened was not so normal.

"Alex?" inquired Rick, bringing me away from that limp down memory lane and back to my kitchen. "Is there a club or bar you'd recommend that's, well, you know, gay? I need to get out ..."

Rick had hung up the phone and was leaning against the counter. I smiled and replied, "Yeah, I can tell you some good places to go. As you can probably gather, I will not be going out tonight. I could be straight, you know."

Rick's eyes brightened and he grinned. "Right, and I'm Condoleeza Rice. Maybe you would go with me ... you know, help me meet some people and show me the cool clubs ... I'm a little bit shy when it comes to going out alone."

It was one-third question, one-third statement, and one-third smart ass, which was unbearably cute. I thought about it for a second and admitted that this was probably a good offer, especially to be seen with a pretty boy like Rick Monette from Atlanta, Georgia. I would probably run across some of Stephen's juvenile friends and they would report the news of my being seen in the presence of a beautiful man. The question though, was the value of being reported in the presence of a new man versus the possibility that Rick could very well be a sex-crazed nut job.

"Hmmm," I said, "I could stand to have a few drinks, especially with a pretty boy like you. Come by around eleven and we'll go."

"Great!" exclaimed Rick, as he moved much closer to me. He came within a few inches of my face, looked down at me and finished his thought, "I love to go out dancing … you never know what may happen."

Rick winked at me and strode out the door. "I'll see you at eleven, then," he said as he turned to go down the stairs.

I smiled again and closed the door, briefly considering that even if he was the lunatic that would strangle me, he was still as hot as hell. I tried to make myself busy fixing something to eat, another battle that had raged after Ayers died, a battle that I managed to keep winning by kicking my own ass swiftly at the gym six days a week, but my thoughts still drifted back to him again. We dated for more than a month before I even let him touch me. Our first date was dinner and a movie, and my salad had edible flowers in it, one of those strange things that stays in your mind, because I kept thinking how out of the ordinary the date really was.

After I dropped him off that night, I made it halfway home only to notice that his jacket was still in the back seat of my car. On our second date, Ayers admitted to leaving the jacket on purpose so that I would have to call him back, a story that was only funny when he was telling it. Of course I replied that I liked the jacket enough to keep it, so my call for the second date was pretty legitimate. Ayers asked me repeatedly to stay the night after the second date but I continually said no. It wasn't because I didn't find him attractive but I just didn't want to spoil the feeling of truly connecting with someone. We were perfect for each other, and, on the night I finally gave in, we found we were perfect for each other in another way. At that time, holding out was a great method for making a little prudishness go a long way.

The night began late, so I went to Ayers' house to pick him up around 11:30. We went to a club for about two hours, sticking close to each other the entire time. I hooked up with some of my hoodlum friends and smoked some great weed, something I did when a vodka martini did not provide quite enough relaxation. Around 1:30, right on the dance floor, I got on my tiptoes and shouted in Ayer's ear, "Take me home. To your house, I mean." We wasted no time on saying goodbyes.

After a few very physical hours and just a tiny nap, I woke up to the sound of water running in the bathroom. I rolled onto my stomach, leaving my butt exposed on purpose, a move that I was convinced was necessary to keep the guy interested. When the water stopped, I felt his presence, watching me from the door of the bedroom.

"You are so hot," Ayers whispered. "What do you want with me?"

He climbed into the bed, opened his arms, and I fell into them, knowing that what happened between us was more than just a passing thing. We slept off and on again that night, and when I woke up in the morning, Ayers was already awake, staring at me, once again telling me how beautiful he thought I was.

After only three months of dating, I asked Ayers to move in with me, lucky that his lease was at an end. I was renting a condo from my mother, who gave us a break on the rent for the first few months when she found out that Ayers had the ability to decorate. The place looked like it was a *Laugh-In* set, with oranges, yellows, and grass cloth wallpaper. He transformed it into a baroque gay show-place, where every wall had a different faux finish and every corner had something ornate to stare at. The day it was considered to be finished, Ayers presented me with my favorite piece of art, a costume sketch of Amneris from a 1960's production of *Aida*, framed in a completely overdone black lacquer and gold frame, hung lovingly, yet obnoxiously, at the foot of the staircase. The frame and its contents were one of the few things that continued to have a physical presence in my life after Ayers died, a constant reminder of those little things that have a lifetime impact like the flowers in the salad.

A drop of water on my hand startled me, this trip down memory lane having caused tears, which was becoming more unusual lately. Because I was a good Southern boy, my tears usually fell in the shower or in my soup, but never when anyone else could see them. My mother always told me two things: never pay full price and never let them see you cry. Since Ayers died, I had not broken her rules.

CHAPTER 3

▼

ENJOY THE STORY

Rick arrived promptly at eleven looking like a Twenty-first Century gay god, dressed completely in black, his tailored shirt drawing attention to his chiseled chest and bulging arms. I wondered for a moment what the rest of it looked like as he walked through the door, his body moving in harmony with the David Benoit CD playing in the background.

"I made some Cosmopolitans," I explained. "I hope you like mixed drinks …"

"I'm best friends with them lately," said Rick with that ever-so sly grin on his face.

Trying not to laugh at this sly attempt at drinking humor, I handed Rick one of my prized deco-martini glasses filled with very light pink liquid, an indication that I had probably made the drinks a tiny bit strong. We moved to the living room and comically sat at opposite ends of the sofa, like an old fashioned courting couple. I turned slightly to my left so I could get a good look, and Rick took a sip of his drink, letting his tongue tickle the rim of the glass before completely lifting it to his lips. My mind whirred with the possibilities of this meeting, then I scolded myself for thinking about it.

After all, I thought, I'm just getting to know a new friend who could be a psychotic murderer.

"So," Rick broke the silence, "where are you taking me tonight?"

"Well," I said, "I thought we could start out at Christina's, which is a smaller bar with a dance floor. Then we can go to Station 69. It's this huge old firehouse that's been, um, well, corrupted. The bartenders dress like firemen, except that they just wear the pants and the suspenders. It's almost more than flesh and blood can handle."

Rick laughed and pitched back his Cosmopolitan. I shrugged and did the same. As my eyes burned from my own concoction, I chuckled and said under my breath: "Nothin' like a girl who can't hold her liquor ... well, I guess it's off to Christina's."

We left the apartment quickly, hoping to avoid any more awkwardness. We rode in the car with the top down, and I sensed that I could get used to people seeing me with this man instead of Disposable Boy.

At Christina's the crowd was under twenty-five and blatantly looking for husbands. We stood at the bar drinking vodka cranberries and talking about everything, including sex with a man and his pierced penis, the tired "I'm a widow" speech, and the fact that Rick was only three years older than me. I began to feel tipsy after the third drink and most certainly felt it was easier to warm up to my new friend, who I was now convinced was not a horny killer. We critiqued the young ones for their apparent clothing whimsies, including low-rider jeans and super starlet wannabes. When we decided to leave "Pee Wee's Playhouse", as Rick named it, for Station 69, I slipped my arm around Rick's waist and we happily walked out to the car. I handed over the keys ceremoniously and declared that I was not in any condition to drive, a sure sign that either the alcohol or I was trusting Rick Monette with the keys to my prized possession.

"I will proudly drive you, sir," Rick announced.

"My hero," I sighed as I plopped into the passenger seat. Suddenly, Rick leaned very close and kissed me on the lips. I was shocked for a moment, but, in my tipsy haze, returned the kiss and put my hand on the back of Rick's neck. I could not believe that I was in a totally different place than I was just a few hours before. Here I was doing things that I had not dreamed of, kissing a stranger in my own car even though my usual loyalty to a boyfriend, even one like Stephen, could not be broken. It was totally impulsive for me to agree to go out with Rick but for some reason I did and was starting to have a good time. I decided to play it cool, to attempt to stay in control, although the devil inside was telling me to take advantage of the situation. Finally, I pulled away and spoke in a near-whisper, hoping the humor in my statement would break the moment.

"Please drive. I do not feel like getting leather burns on my knees in the back seat of my own car. I may be easy but one must have standards, you know." When I said this I smiled at Rick, who grinned back.

"You're pretty cute," Rick said. "And I think you know it. What's hiding in that head of yours?"

"Once again, doctor," I bitched, "drive *my* car to the club. Maybe someday you'll find out what's in this head of mine."

The lot was full at Station 69, so we had to park a block away and walk. When we got through the door, we went straight to the bar and downed more cocktails and a couple of shots, then we hit the dance floor. The music was good, the boys were pretty, and I had somehow ended up with the prettiest one in the place, although I would pay for the drinks with a headache in the morning. We started dancing in a group, then moved off to dance by ourselves, when Rick finally grabbed me and pulled me close. A young grunge boy was watching from the sidelines as I slipped Rick's shirt off and hung it out of my back pocket, another unusually bold move. This whole scene was completely surreal to me, because most of my club nights lately were spent with Stephen and his friends, feeling like a fish out of water. In fact, before I met Stephen, I didn't darken the door of a hardcore dance club for at least a couple of years, spending Saturday nights either alone or on dead-end dates with guys I wasn't even sure I wanted to be out with. Now, as if I was acting in a weird music video, I was actually dancing with an awesome guy who was closer to my own age. If Rick had not ended up in my apartment earlier, I probably would not have left home, most likely curling up with a book until I fell asleep.

The glistening sweat ran into the muscular crevices of Rick's torso and ended up on me as we kept dancing. The young grunge boy intercepted us when we moved off of the floor in search of water. He had a cute face but snarled like the neighborhood bully, and his hair would have been great if it hadn't been so greasy. There was a tattoo of something crawling up his arm, but I decided not to try to figure out what it was for fear of getting the spins.

"Hey, Alex," he said. "I talked to Stephen earlier. You didn't waste time gettin' here, did you?"

To me, it sounded as if grunge boy had said, "Zhoo dint wase tam gittin here, did zhoo?" because his tongue was pierced, a personal statement that had fortunately passed me by, although many other personal statements had not, such as rolled jeans, skater hair cuts, belly button rings, and even parachute pants.

"Are they serving milk tonight?" I said snottily. "And I thought even to a bird-brain that it was obvious Stephen and I aren't joined at the hip. Later little one."

Rick was laughing heartily at my cold-headache cattiness. He looked into my eyes and froze, confident that his glare would stop me in my tracks. I rooted to the spot for a moment then looked away. I glanced at my watch and then turned back to Rick.

"I'm ready to go," I slurred, "because I'm drunk and when I'm drunk I'm mean. I don't want to be mean to anyone else."

I fancied myself a male Margo Channing, glamorously splashing martinis around and saying things like "dahling" and laughing a throaty laugh at other people's expense. When I started feeling this way, it was usually time to bow out gracefully before things got ugly.

"I'm ready too," answered Rick, "and I think I'll drive. It's only a couple of blocks."

The short drive back was quiet as both of us planned silently what we would or would not do. I was also fighting my usual good-versus evil battle, silently reading myself the riot act for getting drunk with someone I hardly knew, but still listening to my voice of reason. There must have been an immediate connection between us if I felt comfortable enough to drink that much. Could it be possible to feel immediately at home with someone brand new again, to have a feeling that was strangely like love at first sight, again? I broke the silence when we arrived at my back door.

"Well, what's the decision? I mean, what are you planning on trying with me?" I smiled my boyish grin as I said this.

"I'm a gentleman," said Rick, "so I'm not going to try anything."

"But," I drawled, "what would you do if you were not a gentleman?"

Rick moved closer and I could smell the mix of liquors on his breath.

"I'd put my arms around you," he whispered as he wrapped his arms around me. "And I'd kiss you again, keeping in mind that we've just met, you have a boyfriend, and for all I know you could be some psycho who's gonna strangle me with the drapes."

Our noses met briefly and then I felt my lips being touched by his. Our bodies pressed together like we were trying to get past each other in a crowded hallway, then suddenly I felt compelled to push Rick away, turning my head to the side. He placed his hand on one side of my face and spoke softly.

"What is it?" he asked.

I felt my face cloud over and I tried hard to enunciate my words fully in my drunkenness. I was trying to figure out how to say that I was shocked over our immediate connection, but I was also afraid that he wasn't feeling the same way. I wanted to tell him that sleeping together this early in the game could be a mistake, not to mention just a slutty thing to do, as if I had never done anything like this in the past. I was walking a fine line between showing my imperfect past and acting like a total prude.

"I really like you, Rick," I said, "and I don't want to spoil those feelings. If you enjoy my company and wanna see more of me, please say so. If you want to do it all night long and have a secret between neighbors, please tell me. I can go along with that but I'll have to turn off my emotions. Oh yeah, and, um, we just met."

The secret between neighbors thing came easily, because I had in some dirty way envied one of my neighbors for having a hot and heavy affair with an upstairs hottie, for being able to get it on easily with someone he could have run into at the mailbox or in the laundry room while sorting dirty underwear. Rick had begun smiling, making his eyes twinkle, and that view of him smacked me with the reality that I did not want this to be a secret between neighbors, that I wanted to see where it might go.

"You're an unusual one," he said. "I really want to see you again. I can wait if you want to. I'm going to Atlanta on Monday to see my parents. I'll be back on Wednesday. Let's talk then."

I wanted him. I was tired of being boxed in by a boy who needed constant attention and care, like a prized orchid. But I knew to savor the moment. Rick turned to leave and leaned over to kiss me on the cheek.

"I'll see you around I'm sure, neighbor," he said.

I closed and locked the door and went straight to the bedroom, undressing completely and falling into bed, more confused than ever. There was something holding me to Stephen, but at the same time I desperately wanted to get rid of him, or maybe it was get rid of the relationship the way it stood at the time. I could not quite come to grips with the fact that I had developed an attraction to a man I had just met, after all, I somehow believed that the instant attraction only happened once in our lives, and Ayers was my one time. This feeling confused me, because if the instant attraction only happened once, the attraction I had for Rick couldn't possibly be real. This had to be an infatuation with a drop-dead gorgeous man who showed the slightest bit of interest in me. Still, that small, foreign voice was telling me to just let it happen. The bitchy part of me wanted to yell "stop!" and send everyone out the door, Disposable Boy and all.

The thought of taking a vow of celibacy and silence actually entered my mind for a moment, then I laughed out loud, knowing that neither had a slim chance of getting past minute one. After Ayers, and even before him, chances were something that stunt pilots took, but not something that I would risk. The safe place I had created for myself was the best place to watch life happening, and, when life happened to me, I would painstakingly analyze it to the point of exhaustion.

Since Ayers, there were no unplanned events, nothing that just occurred because I let it occur, no chances that were taken because they might be a doorway to something fantastic.

Then, for a brief second, spurred on by the events of the evening, I thought about what it would be like to take a chance, to watch my own story unfold for once without worrying about where the chance would take me and actually enjoying it.

CHAPTER 4

▼

SEX AND THE NOT-SO-SINGLE MAN

I woke up to the sound of the key in the back door. I rolled over and sat up on both elbows, watching the room spin from my earlier indulgence.

I've got to take that key away from him, I thought.

I heard Stephen stumble through the kitchen and saw him through the dim light from the street with my half-closed left eye, when he paused in the doorway and began to strip his clothes off where he stood. I watched this, a new world speed record for getting naked, while still pretending to sleep. Stephen paused for a second, watching me. He then walked over, quietly got into the bed, turned opposite me, and sighed long and hard. I could feel his heart racing, probably from the coke he had sniffed earlier.

I rolled over and got close to Stephen's ear, where I whispered, "What did you do tonight?" even though I pretty much knew the drill.

It was a typical night for Stephen. He went to his mother's house, stopping to make sure she didn't need anything, and then called his brother. Andrew came over to check up on his mother but also to bring more cocaine for Stephen, which was now the standing order. When they were sure their mother was asleep, they did a few lines outside by the pool, in an affluent neighborhood where the drug abuse was rampant but the tax revenue was much higher, a guaranteed cop stopper. The brothers had a few drinks until Stephen got a call from the young grunge boy who'd caught Rick and I dancing at Station 69. From there, the group of grungy gay boys, minus Andrew and plus a few hits of Ecstasy, went to a bar, another dance club, and a gay stripper bar, where a sleek dancer with nipple rings mesmerized Stephen through the better part of two vodka tonics and twenty one-dollar bills.

"Shit, dude," snorted Stephen. "I did Ex because I thought I'd run into you."

That comment alone made me feel yet again that I was just wasting time with Stephen, that the idiotic assumption he just made was a painful indication of exactly how our relationship stood. He actually expected to run into me at one of the clubs, as if his being absent for once would cause me to choose going out specifically to look for him. It made me a little angry, so I grabbed Stephen's shoulder and rolled him over on his back, a sexually comical move that would have made it to the cutting room floor for even the cheapest porno film. He fought for a second and then dramatically gave up. We gyrated violently against each other as I tried my best to kiss him sloppily, the two male egos fighting it out under the sheets. Then I thought about how much Stephen was beginning to repulse me, but by that time I was so horny that it just didn't matter anymore. I tongued my way across his smooth chest, proudly keeping a straight face, and then felt something cold against my lips. I sat up abruptly.

"You got your freakin' nipple pierced? When did you do that?" I inquired.

The idea of body piercings had always appeared to me as an expression of individuality, of art attached to life, of a way to say "I'm different and proud". I once pierced my belly button and left it there for a couple of years, a display of my own rebellion against my straight religious upbringing although Ayers insisted it did nothing to improve my attractiveness. Looking at Stephen, with his Prince Albert penis piercing and now a nipple, I wondered if this was a desire to stand out, a desire to get attention, or a desire to mutilate himself. I could sense that this was someone who had been slowly going off course but who was now spinning rapidly out of control, doing things like getting pierced for the wrong reasons. I felt like I had to do something, but then again, I wasn't even sure what my feelings for Stephen really were.

"Oh, can it, bitch," Stephen's voice rose. "I can do whatever I want." He had a way of going from grunge dude to overly queeny in three and a half seconds when he got upset.

"Of course you can, baby," I said in an icy tone as I grabbed his chin and shook it a little. "Just don't get your metal tangled."

"Bastard," choked Stephen. "I heard you were out with some hottie …"

"He's a friend of mine," I replied. "Now would you just chill out? Do you want some pot? I've got a joint rolled."

I immediately felt guilty for offering this, something that I kept around just in case I needed to lighten the mood, especially lately. I also wondered what Rick Monette would say about me smoking a little hooch every now and then, which was an unusual thought in this circumstance. My trio of shrinks would have called me an enabler, helping Stephen into and out of his addiction with the pot, when really all I was trying to do was take the edge off what was going to be a difficult situation. The time for apologies, I thought, would be later. Now was the time to do what needed to be done. Stephen sat up as I went over to the dresser and rummaged around for the joint. I lit it and took a long drag, holding in the smoke as long as I could. I exhaled and passed the joint to Stephen, who was now sitting on the edge of the bed. We smoked it in silence, staring at each other. Smoking pot usually just brought me down a few pegs but, then again, I was usually in calm surroundings on the rare occasions when I smoked it. Now would be a good time to give it up, so I decided then and there not to refill the stash once it was gone. I could sense that Stephen was getting tired of the game, so I numbed my mind and we did what we had been best at, although I avoided the newly pierced nipple. After a few minutes, I usually began to enjoy the sex with him as long as I kept my thoughts and emotions out of it. Too soon it was over and we lay panting for some time until he sat up, reached over to the nightstand, and lit a cigarette.

The blue smoke circled his head, drawing attention to his messy hair. The bedroom smelled like stale pot, cigarette smoke, and sex, which would have been perfect for Station 69 but not for my house, and I realized again at that moment how Stephen repulsed me, how his way disgusted me. I had been so attracted to him, his youth, his smile, and definitely his body. When he first started sleeping over, I always tried to wake up before he did so that I could watch him, stretching and flexing his muscles. After a few weeks, he got to the burping and farting stage before I could even think about getting there, another indication that the relationship was probably doomed. He could come in the apartment after work, strip down to his boxer briefs, looking so hot and sexy, drink a Diet Coke and then belch in sentences like a teenager. When his drug use became obvious, the attraction went further away, the first time he did coke in front of me being the last time.

There were still moments of clarity, where I saw the person behind all of the disgusting habits that would have been transparent if the relationship was right. I began to blame myself for the feeling of disgust because Stephen was the youngest person I had ever dated. In my impulsive reaction to suddenly finding a twenty-two year old after me I may have overlooked my own standards when it came to age and maturity. The relationship had to change, but I could not figure out how.

He looked down at his feet, as if he could tell what I was thinking. I sat up and moved over to him, draping my arm over his shoulder, like that empty gesture could help. I held out my hand for a drag on the cigarette and he handed it to me.

"Are you, like, seeing this new guy?" he asked.

"No," I said, "but you and I really need a break. You should find somebody like you, not like me."

When I said this, he glared over at me and I saw the tears well up in his eyes, something he could do on command or if slightly moved, an act I could never quite decipher unless it was planned. Once, Stephen was driving me somewhere in the Lexus IS 300 his mother bought for him as a graduation gift when we were pulled over by a female cop.

"Watch this," he had said, and proceeded to cry on command as the cop came to the window, blabbering some story about how he was stressed out and had just come from visiting his senile grandmother at the retirement home.

The long tip of ash on the cigarette finally snowed itself to the floor, but I saw that it was because Stephen's hand was shaking.

Oh no, I thought. "Here we go with the last scene in *Gone With the Wind*. Frankly my dear …"

"What the hell am I gonna to do now?" he whined.

"Stephen," I replied, "you're a grown man with a real job and a place of your own. You have friends and a family that need you."

He started to cry, the welled-up tears now falling, and again I really couldn't tell if it was real or not. He looked pitiful, sitting naked on the side of the bed with a smoldering cigarette, dark circles around his eyes.

"I'm sorry," I said, "but I thought you understood that this couldn't go on forever. Now tell me the truth, are you in love with me?"

"Well, no," he sniveled. "I mean, I don't know. I like hanging out with you."

"Baby," I said, "you like my money and the sex. You know you'd rather be hanging out with your friends and dating guys your age who want to keep up with you."

I made a mental note that this was possibly rock bottom, having a break-up talk while still naked, while the post-sex cigarette was still actually being smoked.

Then Stephen spoke slowly, although quickly resolved to the conversation we had just had. "Um, can I stay tonight?"

I knew that was coming, and out of my sympathy for the poor guy I somehow managed to say yes and pulled him onto the bed with me, tucking him in. I felt responsible for him at that very moment, something I had tried extremely hard to avoid. That's when the thought entered my mind that our relationship was wrong because he needed me as a friend and not a sex partner, so maybe my feelings for him were moved by friendship. I still needed him to be gone, even for a few days, to really sort out my true feelings.

When we woke up, the light was streaming through the windows and the room had begun to heat up. Stephen looked angelic as he stirred, probably a little confused about the night before. He rolled over and looked at me, giving me sad yet surprisingly bedroom eyes. When he rolled over, I could feel him pressing against me. I tried to hide my usual morning condition, still relieved that I started one more day with the same problem, but he caught on, smiled really big and laughingly said, "One more for the road?"

I didn't really feel like making cheap sex as we had the night before, but I let him climb on top of me anyway, since I had always been one for a last ditch effort. When I made my last ditch effort at being straight, way back in high school, I made out with Brandy Willis in the back seat of my car for about thirty seconds, until we both started laughing. Stephen started kissing me and then we lay there thrashing against each other like fish in a net. This must have gone on for about twenty minutes, a record for Disposable Boy. Even afterwards, I still felt that twinge of responsibility. I stayed in bed while he showered and dressed, and then I got up and put on my boxers to walk him to the door.

He turned at the door and said, "Can I call you sometime?"

I tried to make my face look sad and answered, "We'll see. I'll see you, okay? Please take care of yourself."

With that, he was gone. I returned easily to the solitude of myself, basking in the warmth of my bedroom alone but worrying if karma would someday be interested in the little saga that had just ended.

CHAPTER 5

▼

WHICH GAME ARE YOU PLAYING?

I hid in my work week until Wednesday, working late and staying at the gym for an extra hour, still hoping to catch a glimpse of Rick, but also trying to stay busy. The summer was in full swing, so the light was good until around 7:30. I got home that Wednesday afternoon around 5:30, when the heat was still shimmering off of the parking lot.

As I got out of the car, Rick approached, a gay guy's wet dream, wearing very brief running shorts and no shirt. I got a much better look at him in the afternoon sun. His stomach was totally ripped, each muscle clearly defined below his perfectly shaped pecs, a slightly hairy treasure trail disappearing into the waistband of his shorts. His shoulders were rounded out and broad, and his skin was smooth, although I wasn't sure if it was naturally that way or if he had a good wax technician. He was just tan enough, and from the look of the brief shorts, tanned just enough all over. Rick walked up with a big grin on his face.

"Hey you," he said. "Wanna go jogging with me? I can see how fit you are, anyway."

Two things came to mind. First, two decent looking guys running in our neighborhood were bound to get some attention. And second, I really didn't know if my repressed hormones could take it. The thought of running with an erection just did not appeal to me.

"Sure," I said quickly. "Let me go change and meet me back here in about fifteen minutes. Is that good for you?"

"I can't wait," he replied.

I nearly tripped up the stairs, I was moving so quickly. I decided on some tired but still cute running shorts and a white cap because my hair was not the sort that stayed put while jogging. Usually, after a run, I resembled a Salem witch after a dipping. I peered out the window to see Rick stretching in the parking lot next to my car. He bent over to touch his toes and his brown back muscles stretched in the sunlight. When he raised himself up, I was drawn once again to that perfect chest and pretty stomach. A pain flashed in the pit of my stomach because I really liked this guy and it looked like he was returning the favor. I was also afraid because I had let the cardio go for a few weeks, just working out with weights three or four times a week. There was nothing more unpleasant than my doing cardio after a long break, huffing and puffing as if every breath would be my last. When I went through a spinning phase a couple of years earlier, my first teacher actually had to stop the class to ask me if I was all right because I was such a mess. The key here would be to hide the misery every step of the way.

When I made it downstairs, we set our watches and started out. I found that, even at his height, Rick Monette stayed in step with my little legs the entire time we ran. We both started to sweat and I noticed that his chest looked even better shiny. We talked some, but mainly ran in silence, the kind of silence that happens between two people who can think on the same wavelength. Men were cruising us in their cars as they drove by, so I really wanted to stop and yell, "Back off, bitches, this one's gonna be mine!" In our short, breathless conversations, Rick displayed a very deadpan sense of humor, something that attracted me to him even more.

"I haven't seen your little boy toy today," said Rick. "Don't tell me you finally got rid of him?" He sounded more hopeful than cynical.

Huffing and puffing, I tried to think of a way to respond nicely. "Well," I replied, "you can only get so much sex. When there's no substance to your relationship, when you can't have a conversation after you do it, what's the use?"

After a few more huffs and puffs, I admitted that I had gotten rid of Stephen, just for good measure.

"Sex is good," he replied, "with the right person."

There was that sideways glance again. Either I was imagining it or he was really throwing out the I'm-gonna-get-you looks. We ran in silence past the golfers and the cruisers and the other runners. When we got back to our building, I was completely exhausted, watching him with such interest the entire time it never occurred to me that I was half dead. We stopped in front of my staircase, bending and stretching the kinks out of our tired legs. Rick looked like Adonis, even after a three-mile run in ninety-degree heat, and his damned hair still looked good, too.

"I've got to have some water," I said, rasping through my dry throat. "You need to come up and get some, too."

He smiled at me through the sweat neatly pouring off of his forehead and gave a gentlemanly sweep of his arm to let me go up the stairway first. Once in my kitchen, I handed him a tall glass of water, which he drank in a few short gulps. I gazed, once again in amazement, at his beautiful body, ridiculously hoping that he was not aware of my stares.

"You," he said emphatically, "look just as good as I do. Stop staring."

I blushed as he gave me that smile again.

"Please have dinner at my place tonight!" he blurted out, then slowed to finish his invitation. "I've planned to cook tonight and I want you to come over. No pressure, though."

No pressure? I thought to myself. No pressure when Mr. Drop Dead Gorgeous asks me to dinner at his house with two hour's notice?

I had been hoping that he would ask me out, but the home cooked meal was a step beyond. He was inviting me inside his home, which was the invitation not only to sample the food but also to see if he was a good housekeeper. I could run my white glove across his coffee table and check out his bedroom. He already appeared to be too good to be true.

"I'd love to," I said. "Did you just assume that I wouldn't have plans?"

"Well, um," he said, and then smiled. "Lookie-here, I just got up the freakin' nerve to ask you out so not fair to string me on!"

"No plans," I replied with a laugh. "I just had to make a fair drama out of the short notice. This is the best thing to happen on a Wednesday in a long time. What time?"

"Seven thirty," he replied. "I haven't cooked for anyone in a while. I better go so I can get things started."

As he walked down the stairs, I watched him again. That body could do no wrong, even sweaty and dirty, and the man behind it was turning out to be just as cool. I locked the door behind him and thought about the cooking. Ayers was a gourmet waiting to happen. Just as MacGyver could make a bomb out of a piece of string and a stick of gum, Ayers could make a gourmet meal out of a piece of stale bread and a frozen chicken breast. He knew that feeding me well was a good staying-point in the relationship, something that Rick seemed to be zeroing in on already. After all, Rick could probably tell that I was no cook from the cleanliness of my kitchen and the unused state of my appliances. I had actually asked my real estate agent to find an apartment with no kitchen to save money and was disappointed to find out that most residences had kitchens. I laughed out loud as I remembered not to judge any new prospective boyfriend by his cooking. But, I could judge him by the coziness of his bedroom and the cleanliness of his home.

I showered quickly and padded into my bedroom closet to find some clothes that would work for a first date. I stood in the closet doorway, wondering if anyone else but Ayers could put up with my closets, arranged by color, each item hung exactly the same distance from the next one, shoes arranged neatly, not touching each other, with their shoe trees inside. I knew exactly where each item was, and when I picked something to wear, it had probably been thoroughly premeditated beforehand. I never allowed Ayers to hang anything in my closet, something he laughingly referred to as "fascist fashions", but it was just one of my peculiarities that he learned to love. Could someone else learn to love those peculiarities, or was he the only one? I picked up the phone to find that there was a new message. Before I dialed my password I knew that it would not be a welcome voice.

"Dude," Stephen's voice sounded tired and bewildered, "I just wanted to see how you're doing. I miss you … I'll change if you want me to. No more drugs. I can get rid of my friends. I just want you …" His voice trailed off. I felt sorry for him immediately, probably the desired effect. The thought of him repulsed me, but the thought of his body made me wonder if I could do without the hot sex for a while.

I decided not to call him just yet. He needed to take some time for himself and I needed to get over the sex addiction of the relationship. Even though it looked like I was moving along with Rick, there was a part of me that could end up in bed with Stephen again if the timing and the light were just right. I hoped that the next time I saw him I would be over him as quickly as he could belch "your mama is a whore" after a few swigs of Diet Coke.

I found my trusty black Armani pullover and Calvin Klein jeans, in their assigned positions, of course, and guessed that dead-of-summer two person dinner parties were pretty casual at Rick's house. I looked like the gay boy-next-door, very presentable, done up well enough for an introduction to Mom and Dad or a hot date. My watch said 7:25 as I spritzed my new Prada cologne, hoping for a scent that was somewhere between sensuous and I-spilled-it-on-myself. A flash of nervousness pulsed through my stomach. What if he wanted to get physical? I wasn't sure what my reaction would be, because between Rick and Stephen, I was beginning to feel like a buck-and-a-quarter tramp. But this relationship had potential. It probably couldn't be like the one I was having with Stephen, useful yet totally disposable. I had to play my cards right on this one. The problem was that I wasn't sure which game I was playing.

CHAPTER 6

▼

EMOTION

I grabbed a bottle of red wine from my bar to present as a gift to Rick, a precious bottle of *Gevrey Chambertin* I'd picked up on a trip to France. The second year after Ayers died, I decided that some travel would help me expand my horizons and continue to recover. The trip I chose was a gay tour group bound for Paris and then the south of France. There were, of course, plenty of single travelers who wanted to hook up for the duration of the trip, but my interest was just not there at the time. I shared a room with a nice old gentleman named Edward who was obviously beyond wanting to hook up with anyone, anyway, so the trip turned out to be very colorful.

On our way back to Paris near the end of the trip we stopped in a small town in Burgundy and a few of us took a tour of one of the many wineries in the region. The winery tour included a tasting, where I found this fantastic red wine. When I went to purchase a few bottles, Edward bought them for me, explaining that he had had a wonderful time on the trip because of me and wanted to thank me. He told me that he rarely found anyone to connect with on these types of trips and that my story touched him, having lost his partner of forty years as recently as I had lost Ayers. Although those two relationships were probably not comparable, Edward and I shared the bond of loss and enjoyed our trip because both of our dead husbands had always wanted to take the trip we were on. So the bottle of wine I picked out for Rick was one of the ones that were saved for special occasions, something I had not had many of in the past few months.

At the exact appointed time, I knocked on Rick's door. I stood there, nice and shiny, with the bottle in one hand, leaning ever-so-nonchalantly on the door-frame. When the door opened, I was immediately breathless by the sight of him, which was becoming a regular occurrence. Rick wore jeans and a tight white t-shirt and was, again, perfect. He smelled of garlic mojo and Gucci Envy at the same time and he was wearing a black apron with the words "Kiss me quick" embroidered across the chest.

"Hey you," he said brightly. "Come on in. I'm still putting stuff away from the move."

I did not know what he was referring to, so I said nothing. The place was immaculate, much like my own. The white glove would pass very easily in Rick Monette's house. He led me through his living room, full of very modern furniture which appeared to have been picked out piece by piece, a sure sign of patience. I quickly flashed back to picking out my living room furniture in one swoop, all mixed and matched by the chain furniture store it came from. He pointed out his spare bedroom, which was really a guest room with his desk and laptop in it, for sudden visits by his parents. Then it was time for the big glimpse, the first sight of Rick's bedroom.

"The bedroom," he said while showing the way, "is always my favorite room in the house. It's sort of like your escape from the real world, so it's got to be over-the-top."

In the middle of the room stood a wrought iron canopy bed, with a gold and black comforter accented by leopard skin, gold, black, and black striped pillows. The canopy was draped in white toile, a gay guy's exotic safari mosquito net, the bed screaming *sensual* so loud I think we both heard it. There were two deco nightstands on either side, the type of smoked brown rounded-corner furniture that Joan Crawford may have had, one complete with a forties-style telephone, and in one corner was an iron candelabra that was taller than me. He had a matching deco dresser with fresh roses on top of it, along with a couple of sterling Tiffany rings, a David Yurman necklace, and collar stays thrown casually around. There was a mirrored vanity tray that reminded me of the one my mother had, and looking carefully, I noticed that Rick's scents were the Envy, a Chanel for men, and the latest Cerrutti. There were candles all over the room, enough candles to have midnight mass, but I noticed that most of the wicks were just black enough and the wax just melted enough to have been burned only once. The art on the walls looked original to my untrained eye, one of the pieces a very light watercolor and ink of bare-breasted women lying around with their cats. This room was certainly an over-the-top escape, a room that two people could make into a romantic love nest. To avoid fainting over all of this, I stupidly spoke up.

"I brought you some wine as a sort of thank-you, welcome to the neighborhood gift," I said, remembering that I had been traipsing around with the bottle. "So put this in your cellar for a special occasion. I schlepped these bottles all the way back from France, you know."

He took the wine and led me into the dining room. The table was set for two, complete with candles, china, and a bouquet of fresh flowers on one plate.

"I wanted to do something charming," said Rick slowly, "so I brought you flowers arranged by yours truly."

"Thanks," I said weakly, "that's really sweet." I felt like I was going to pass out if I didn't grab him and kiss him.

"Screw the dinner and let's get to dessert," my inner slut said, but thankfully this time not out loud.

The smells coming from the kitchen were mouth-watering, and his iPod was cranking out *"Zing Went the Strings of My Heart"*. I sat down in my chair, picking up the bouquet to give it a sniff, while Rick went back to the kitchen and pulled something out of the oven. His body was so fluid and graceful, and he moved around in the kitchen like the whole thing had been choreographed.

"It won't be another minute," he yelled over the music. "I fixed roasted chicken with vegetables and a spinach salad. I hope you eat meat, by the way."

My eyes widened at the meat comment, as Rick was standing in the doorway of the dining room. He had a serving platter in one hand and a ceramic bowl in the other. He sat down and began dishing out chicken, potatoes, green and red peppers, and spinach salad. When he finished with my plate, which could have been a magazine cover, he looked up suddenly.

"I almost forgot the wine!" he said loudly, which nearly made me jump. "I mean, what's roasted chicken on a hot summer night with no cold pinot?"

I smiled at him, still speechless. I watched his backside as he walked over to the fridge, the kind of butt you could put your hands on, and then to top it off, the muscles in his arms worked and flexed as he pulled the cork out of the bottle. Every part of his body was in synchronization with the other. He ate very deliberately, appearing to savor each bite and using his pretty lips to drink his wine. This was one of his ways that had already begun to stay with me, that light flick of the tongue over the rim of the glass before enfolding it with those pink lips. If men could have orgasms visually without touching themselves, I could have had one just watching Rick drink.

"You've never really said exactly what you do for a living," said Rick after a moment. "I've heard you talk about your job but it's still not clear."

"Well," I said, choosing my words carefully in my mind, "I'm an investment broker for James, Robertson, & Savage. It pays well but it gets kind of boring. My department is cool, though, we handle international clients."

"Very interesting and businesslike," he drawled through his wine-soaked lips. "Don't sell yourself short. It sounds very respectful."

"Well, actually," I said shyly, "I'm a Vice President with the firm. It looks good on paper, anyway."

"A Vice President?" he asked. "You look too young to be titled."

I smiled and took another bite of spinach salad.

"You told me you run your parent's business," I said, recalling a brief conversation at the club the other night, "but what business are they in?"

"You know Gilroy's Florists?" he asked. "We just bought them a few months ago. I'm sort of the general manager."

The visual orgasm I had been having suddenly intensified. The florist he was referring to was a huge operation, handling retail, wholesale, and delivery of flowers, plants, and custom arrangements, and had been around for years. Every respectable society member used Gilroy's for everything from weddings to dinner parties to funerals.

"We were a normal family for quite a few years," Rick said. "Mom stayed home with us kids and Dad worked in the accounting division of a bank. When I was old enough to let myself in after school, Mom decided to go back to work in a floral shop. Like any good Southern girl, she'd learned that skill way back when and then studied design in college. She got her degree in fine arts."

Mrs. Monette went to work for a small mom and pop florist, he explained, turning out luscious creations that ended up in the best homes in Atlanta. When the mom and pop decided to retire, the Monettes bought the business with the expectation that Mrs. Monette would run it. They reasoned that it just couldn't get any bigger than it was, so Rick drove the delivery van after school and helped his mother design new arrangements. As business picked up, the one shop florist grew into a conglomeration of new and acquired stores, with Mrs. Monette moving from the design table to the office upstairs, presiding over a floral empire. Rick entered college to study business just as his father left his job in accounting to become the Chief Financial Officer of the newly formed company. Rick worked summers and holidays, learning the business while getting his degree, constantly returning home with new ideas, plans, and theories on the operation. After graduation, Rick went to work for Monette Floral as the Chief Operating

Officer, and business was booming so much that he got the salary to go with it. His parents treated him like any other executive and he even called them by their first names at the office, an arrangement that lasted until Rick decided to expand out of state. Rick kept tabs on what the other big floral companies were doing, and when a chink in the armor appeared at Gilroy's in Memphis, he pulled the executives together and got them to vote for the acquisition, with his transfer as one of the conditions.

"My parents are pretty much ready to retire and are expecting me to take over as the big chief at Monette Floral," Rick said. "One of my first acts as C.O.O. is to move our headquarters here to Memphis to make them more centrally located."

So Rick was not only gorgeous and financially independent, but a superior businessman, too.

"What's the catch?" I asked out loud then caught myself. "Oh my God, did I say that out loud? Oh well, why in hell don't you have a husband?"

Rick laughed and then his eyes momentarily lost their twinkle.

"Long story," he said, dryly. "Maybe if you're good I'll tell it to you."

As we finished our dinner, I could not take my eyes off of Rick's lips, which were telling me several things: he took care of his skin, he could kiss, and he could probably suck the chrome off of a 1977 Buick.

Rick got up and began clearing the table, so I immediately helped him, walking over to the sink with as many dishes as possible. I opened the dishwasher and started rinsing plates, but he slid up beside me and put his arm around my waist, giving me a long squeeze. He put his mouth right next to my ear and whispered into it, "Those soft hands shouldn't do dishes, Marge. Have a seat in the living room. Pour yourself some port."

I steeled my eyes on his and in that cold-headache voice he seemed to like so much, I answered, "I insist. A proper guest always cleans up after himself." Enough port would have made me horizontal in ten seconds flat, anyway.

Rick pulled me closer and kissed me ever so lightly on the lips, using the other hand to brush my cheek. I turned to him, leaving the water running, and put my arms around his shoulders. We embraced and kissed again, still lips only and in slow motion. When the kissing stopped, we were both riveted to the spot, looking deeply into each other's eyes. I didn't know what to say or do, but Rick broke the silence.

"Why don't we leave these dishes," he said, "and go have some port. I'll clean up later."

He released me and I stood there in a stupor while he smiled again. He took me by the hand and led me to the living room, where a small, neatly stocked bar cart waited. I sat down on the sofa and watched his butt again. He turned around and handed me a glass of port and then sat down next to me on the sofa.

"So, Alex," he said. "Tell me more about your, um, life."

He was probing for more information about Ayers, but as people normally behaved, did not want to bring up the subject directly. Mercifully, the phone rang as I was about to answer. Rick reached over to the end table and answered it.

"Hello?" he said disgustedly. "Oh, hi Mom. Yeah, I've got company."

He shrugged, winked at me, and walked away, taking the phone with him. I sipped my drink and thought about Ayers again, Rick's guest bedroom having reminded me. We had overnight visitors every once and a while, and I remembered when Ayers' best friend from Florida came to visit. She was a hair stylist, so gay men were naturally her friends and she had put up with many of her gay men's natural adventures. The rooms in our house were arranged so that the guestroom door faced our bedroom door. The first night she was there, Ayers decided that he was in the mood, regardless of whether she would hear or not. I tried to fight him off, but as usual could not resist him. We made enough noise to wake the neighborhood, knocking glasses off the nightstands and rattling the walls. After a few minutes of silence, his friend knocked on the door.

"Boys," she laughed, "you've got to give me a lesson in the morning, because whatever you were doing to each other must have been spectacular."

She closed the door as Ayers and I looked at each other. He was red in the face for a moment and then we both burst into wild laughter, rolling all over the bed, throwing pillows. It was another one of those things that seemed insignificant at the time but stayed in my memory.

"Sorry, Alex," Rick's voice interrupted my thoughts. "I have to talk to Mom when she calls."

Rick was looking down at me and smiling. The blank stare on my face seemed to confuse him, and he suddenly got this overly concerned look on his face.

"Oh my God," he said. "I'm so sorry for bringing that up and then leaving you alone!"

"Let me make one point," I declared forcefully. "I do not want pity from you or anyone else. That's the trouble with us fags—we all want to dole out sympathy for the drama value."

Rick looked as if he was going to laugh.

"I'm sorry," I said. "I get kind of opinionated."

Rick smiled again. "No kidding. You were saying?"

"Well," I began to recount the story, "he was fine and then he started feeling tired. He kept calling in to work, staying home, sleeping a lot. I thought he was just in a run-down phase. Anyway, he went to the doctor, who told him he looked fine."

"Doctors," said Rick. "What do they really know anyway?"

Ayers then developed back pain and even had trouble walking, I explained, which he at first believed was a back injury. When he went to the doctor again, the asshole immediately decided that Ayers most likely had AIDS, an assumption that some doctors tended to make when confronted with gay men with unexplained symptoms. The test proved negative, so the doctor pronounced that it must have been rheumatoid arthritis. Of course, this process took months, months that were just taking his life away.

I took him to the emergency room one night, all six feet of Ayers literally crying from the pain in his back and legs, and still nothing from the doctor. Finally, I went home one day to find him on the sofa, slumped over in a daze. Something was obviously very wrong because he had knocked a flowerpot out of a window, having fell into it a few hours earlier. The usually fanatically clean Ayers had left the dirt, crushed flowers, and pieces of terracotta lying on the floor, and really didn't seem to know what was going on. That night was the longest night of my life, sitting next to him in the emergency room while he went in and out of consciousness, babbling incoherently about all kinds of things. One blood test made the determination that his mystery illness was leukemia that had set up shop in his spine and had rapidly spread, his demented state due to a malfunctioning kidney caused by the gradual shutdown of his organs. The oncologist who attended him told me immediately to call his family, to get them there as quickly as possible, as he might not make it through the night, but he did. I spent the next eight days on a sofa in the intensive care waiting room, being herded like a cow into the unit to visit Ayers for the allotted fifteen minutes, not even enough time to take care of the things he needed that the harried staff just could not do for him.

Those eight days were spent in near panic, every time a page went for assistance in one of the ICU bays we thought it was for him. We watched as families were called on to visit outside of normal visiting hours, a sure sign that their loved one was on the way out, and fought the terror of thinking the same thing would happen to us. Ayers received heavy chemo and somehow managed to pull through, his spine permanently damaged and his ability to walk impaired.

After a month in the hospital, he was allowed to go home. His doctors did not tell us at the time that his leukemia was fatal in the majority of its cases, but kept telling us that their plan was to administer chemotherapy at certain intervals.

Those few months were hell, Ayers unable to take care of himself and sicker than I had ever seen anyone in my life. As I recounted the story, mechanically, Rick seemed to be in complete understanding.

"It looked like he had a chance, but three months later he was gone," I said. "Just like that. I mean I knew he was dying, but he didn't accept it until he got really sick, in the last three days. I've been semi-alone since then, because Disposable Boy doesn't really count. Not much else to tell."

"But," replied Rick, "what was he like?"

"It's hard to sum up, really," I said. "He was gorgeous, funny, smart, loyal, great in bed. But, as you get to know me, you'll get to know him. I guess he'll always be a part of me somehow. You can't forget your first love."

When I met Ayers, I had been with other guys and had dated some, but those relationships always seemed to hit a wall after a few weeks. I began to doubt my own ability to love someone, to achieve some sort of intimacy. Before him, I had not known a true romantic love. I had known the love of my family and friends but never the dry throat, butterflies, and insomnia kind of love. With Ayers, I couldn't see anything else but him. I couldn't wait to be around him, I lived to hear his voice and to feel his arms around me. Even though it hit me at a time when I was much less mature, it was still my first love. I wondered often how many people kept their first love, how many people died in bed next to the person who was their first love, years and years after they realized it was the first love. When Ayers marched into the picture, I had not felt like that before and wondered if I would ever feel like that again.

"That seems pretty reasonable," Rick replied. "Mine just left me, that's all. I mean, he's still alive and all but he told me he never wanted to see me again. He wasn't my first love, anyway. That's the long story, though." Rick laughed.

"Am I being good enough to hear it?" I asked.

Rick leaned closer and kissed me again, this time letting his lips linger near mine. He looked at me as if he was trying to make a decision, as if his mouth was poised to say something. Then he pulled me close and held me to him, a gesture which seemed like something he would only do to his husband, not a guy he met just a couple of weeks before. I felt like someone had stolen my vocal chords. Rick sighed heavily and got up from the sofa.

"Can I refill that port for you?" he asked in his best air-hostess voice. "Or are you okay until we land?"

He was smiling at me again. It really seemed to me that this man already had a hold on me, that if he kissed me again and then asked me to get in bed with him, I would have gone on autopilot at that moment because the attraction between us was incredible. I looked at the clock on the wall and knew that I would need to be going home.

"Actually," I said, "I really need to be going. I've got to get my beauty sleep. It's 9:30. You're a fabulous host, though."

When Disposable Boy wasn't around, my spinster waking life ended around ten, where I spent an hour reading in bed, by myself, trying hard to take the stress off of the day. I was not ready to give up my spinster hours after one date, so I worked to excuse myself. Rick leaned forward like he wanted to kiss me again, but I let him give me a peck on the cheek instead. I smiled back at him and gave a simple explanation. "If you kiss me again, I'll be naked on your coffee table."

Rick let out a "hmm" and then got up, holding his hand out to mine. He gave me that lost-boy look again and spoke, "Can we get together again in a couple of days? I hope you want to see me again."

"Absolutely," I answered, trying not to sound desperate, "and since I'm not much of a cook I'll either order something in or we can go out to dinner. Drop by if you get a chance. I'll try to keep my clothes on just in case I have to get the door."

I wanted to kiss him again but I knew what that would do to me. As I walked down the stairs, I felt that soulful sensation that I had only felt once before.

CHAPTER 7

▼

TO THE RESCUE

I locked all the doors when I got back to my apartment, slipped out of my summer dinner clothes and into my silk kimono, an item I had not really used since Ayers died. I selected a bottle of cold white wine and opened it, hoping that a glass would settle me down.

I was just about to reach half a bottle when my cell phone rang. When I answered, Stephen spoke in a choking, garbled voice that sounded unnaturally calm.

"Alex, it's Stephen," he said, using my name instead of "Dude" for the first time in quite a while. "Mom died. She's still here in the house. I don't know what to do …"

I was shocked for a moment, not only at the news of his mother's death but also because he sounded so terrible. I really didn't know what to say. When Ayers died he was in the hospital and we all knew he was dying. Stephen's mother had apparently been doing well and she was at home.

"Are you there at the house," I asked, my voice trembling, "or are you out on your cell?"

"I'm in the house," he replied, choking but obviously past tears, sounding totally strung out.

"Tell me what I should do, Alex," he said, his voice pitifully weak.

"Listen, I'm going to come over there. Call 911 and tell them. They'll send whoever needs to be there. Don't leave. I'll be over in a few minutes."

"Hurry!" he shouted. "I'm scared!"

As soon as I clicked off, my phone rang again.

"Hey sexy," Rick growled. "I saw your light on and I wanted to say good-night."

"Thanks," I said, still in a daze. "Stephen just called. His mother died. He wants me to help him."

"God, how'd you get so lucky? Do you want me to come with you?"

"No. He just can't do anything by himself. He sounded like a drunk five year old a few minutes ago, if you can believe that."

"Call me if you need me. I'll be around."

"Thanks. Goodnight, Rick."

I got dressed and hurried out the door. The night air was heavy and sticky, the tangible humidity of a typical Southern summer. Driving by Rick's apartment, I saw that his bedroom light was still on. When I rounded the corner near Stephen's family home, I saw the police car parked in the driveway, with an officer inside filling out papers. I strode by him cautiously and pushed the front door open to find Stephen sitting in the formal front parlor with his head in his hands, wearing wide leg pants and a dirty white t-shirt. His hair was greasy and flattened on his head and his eyes were dazed and confused, much more than usual. He looked up the minute I walked through the door and ran quickly to me. I had no choice but to hold him because he basically collapsed when my arms went around him.

"Did you do what I said?" I asked when he finally stopped crying.

"Yes," he replied. "The cop says the ambulance is on the way. She was fine, Alex. I just don't understand."

Something told me that Mrs. Clark had not been fine and she just didn't want to cause any more trouble for her already troubled sons. I wondered if Mr. Clark would be coming with his new wife, a strangely dishy thought at a really bad time. As it turned out, the night Stephen came out to his parents was the night that Mr. Clark promised his then-mistress that he would tell his wife about them, and ask for a divorce. After screeching out of the driveway in his Benz, Mr. Clark drove over to West Memphis, Arkansas and back, a trip of about an hour. When he got home, he openly blamed his wife for making Stephen gay, and then blamed them both for the mistress. He ended the marriage then and there, and twenty-one year old Stephen heard the whole thing, taking on the blame for breaking up his parents' marriage. Mr. Clark had had the mistress for a couple of years, a younger woman who happened to be at the right place at the wrong time. Now, after a short period of time, his ex-wife was dead. Stephen held on to me for several minutes and I really did feel sorry for him, looking so small and uncertain in that big house. I saw the lights from the ambulance and asked him quickly, "Where is she?"

"In her bedroom," he replied blankly.

It seemed extremely morbid to think about it, but I knew exactly where that bedroom was. When Mrs. Clark was doing well on her treatments, she went to Biloxi to see her family. Stephen and I messed around endlessly in that master suite in the bed, on the floor, in the shower, and in the oversized Jacuzzi tub. I was a little bit grossed out over it for a second, not only over the sheer morbidity of the whole thing, but also over the fact that I had let myself become so trashy. Before I met Stephen, I never would have imagined having sex in a boyfriend's parent's house. When Ayers and I visited his family, I always told him no, that sex under your parents' roof was as close to blasphemy as you could get. Then I felt grief. She was always very open and accepting of me, almost like a friend, she trusted me and hoped that I would help Stephen get his life together. I felt grief not only for her but also because I felt guilty for enabling Stephen's disgusting habits with my own disgusting habits. I was no stranger to grief, although this was a little different. I had never really stopped grieving for Ayers, it was just a scaled-down grief that comes with time, the hole in my soul still present but covered over. I was so tired of feeling grief at that point, but I saw that choices led me from one point to another and the feelings that came along in between those points were a direct result of those choices. I chose to swing all the way to the other side of my circus tent, doing things with Stephen that I had never even thought of before, allowing things to happen that I was previously opposed to. Grief also made me lonely, so I went along with Stephen just to ensure that I could again hear someone else breathing next to me at night.

The ambulance guys came through the door and I led them to the bedroom. I didn't go inside but told them that she had had cancer and was very sick anyway. They left me to go in, and I turned around and went back into the parlor. Stephen's father arrived along with the new Mrs. Clark. I could tell he dyed his gray hair in the hope of appearing younger, but he acted old. I think he had loved the elder Mrs. Clark and was obviously shaken by her sudden death. I nodded to them both as I came back into the room.

"Mr. Clark, Mrs. Clark," I said politely, having only met them a couple of times.

"Alex," said Mr. Clark in response.

The young Mrs. Clark came over to me and planted one on my cheek, saying simply, "Hi Alex. Thanks for coming. Is he okay?"

Stephen's personality and his ability to charm anyone when he had to paid off, because it was obvious that young Mrs. Clark was concerned about his well-being, more than her husband. The new Mrs. Clark was in her forties and had lived in the area for years, making friends with every gay decorator and hairstylist in town, so a gay stepson was not a stretch. Mr. Clark came over at that point.

"Alex," he said sternly, "I'll take care of the arrangements. You take care of Stephen. He's high as kite and doesn't need to be in the way. Take him away from here and make him call me in the morning."

I nodded, but apparently Stephen had not been able to tell his dad that we were no longer together. And of course it had never occurred to Mr. Clark that his son had served as a stud, someone to help another man get off and nothing more, which would have been a further disappointment. Why did they all look to me as his protector? I walked over to the sofa, sat down next to Stephen and put my arm around his shoulder, honestly wanting him to know that he was not alone. My feelings for him began to unwind there on the sofa, feelings that were telling me to deal with him and try to get him through this mess.

"Stephen," I said clearly and firmly, "your dad is going to take care of everything. You need to come with me, okay? I'll take you home and then you can find out what's going on in the morning."

"Okay," he said softly, then started crying again. He laid his head on my shoulder and began sobbing violently, a genuine yet most likely chemically induced freak-out. Mr. Clark looked over with the quiet disapproval I had seen the few times I met him, and young Mrs. Clark looked on with sympathy. I got up, pulled Stephen to his feet, and prodded him toward the door before they could bring his mother past. I nodded quickly to the Clarks and pushed Stephen out the door, where he mechanically stumbled to the car and got in, putting his head back on the rest. I started the car and screeched out of the driveway, debating whether to take him to his apartment or put him to sleep on my sofa.

We pulled up to my apartment and I looked over at him, out cold. I don't know what he did or who with, but it had done a number on him because I tried to wake him and he wouldn't budge. He was breathing normally and even had a little trickle of spit on his mouth, a final gross out for the evening. I would not be able to get him up the stairs by myself, so I boldly picked up my cell and hit Rick's number, which had already made it into my phonebook.

"Hello?" Rick sounded surprised.

"Rick," I said urgently, "it's Alex. Disposable Boy has literally passed out cold in my car. I can't take him home. Can you come down and help me get him upstairs?"

"Wow," he said, "I haven't seen this much drama since I fell off the jungle gym in third grade. Give me a second, okay?"

A moment later, Rick came walking over and his eyes widened at the sight of Stephen.

"*This* is Disposable Boy?" he asked, having humorously taken license on Stephen's nickname.

"Trust me," I said, "it was better sober and not out cold. Did you come to help me or critique my choice of past boyfriends?"

"Down girl," he retorted. "I'll get one side and you get the other."

We picked Stephen up and fairly easily carried him to each landing on the staircase. When we got him through the door, I nodded toward the sofa. I pulled Stephen's grungy t-shirt off and then went for his shoes, and out of sheer meanness, wrestled with his limp body to get his jeans down and off of him, revealing black boxer briefs. As long as I didn't think about how disgusting he was, I was still a tiny bit attracted to his body. It didn't last long when Rick came back in the room carrying a glass of water, which he handed to me without a word, a signal of his beautiful simplicity, knowing that a little water might save the day. While I was drinking, he went over and stood next to Stephen, then gently pushed him on his back, turning his head slightly to the left.

"He needs to have his head turned in case he pukes," he explained, "so he won't choke."

I had to laugh. Here were two thirty-something men practicing college years, drunk frat boy medicine on a guy who was high but had probably not had a drop of alcohol.

A mischievous smile crossed Rick's face. He reached down, pulled the waistband of Stephen's boxer briefs open, and peered in to get a look. I stood there, stupefied.

"Well," he said with a laugh, "I've never seen a real one with a piercing before. Looks painful. How did that feel?"

"I'd rather not talk about it," I snapped, angry again. "I'm sick of this shit. I can't take care of him."

Rick came over, hugged me tight, pushing my face into his chest. I put my arms around him and just stood there, trembling from being close to him and also from the drama that had just halfway been completed on my part. He looked down and his lips were a few inches from my face.

"Why don't I sleep here tonight? If Disposable Boy wakes up, I'll help him out," he whispered, as if there was a possibility we could wake Stephen up. "You look like shit. Don't be so upset about it. We gays are family, whether we want to be or not. The good among us have to take care of the stupid. It's nature's way."

He acted as if he was going to go over to the loveseat, but I held his hand.

"You can sleep with me," I said meekly, and led him to the bedroom, where the bed was already unmade. I sat down and stripped off my clothes, and it was a damned good thing that I wore my best pair of sexy briefs. Rick did the same, following my lead. We slipped into bed and Rick opened his arms to me as an "it's safe" gesture.

"You never told me about your first love," I said quietly, chatting to him like pillow talk between us was a normal thing.

"I don't think I've had that pleasure yet," he replied.

He enfolded me in his muscular arms, my head coming to rest quickly on his chest. I was asleep within minutes, not an easy task for someone as high strung as me, someone who worried about snoring or farting in my sleep. This was a peace I had not felt in a long time.

CHAPTER 8

▼

DIRECTION

I woke up to the sound of the alarm going off and saw that Rick really did sleep in my bed, that it was not a dream. He looked so sweet, lying there turned toward me, starting to stir. He woke up, looked at me, smiled, and then stretched, flexing his ample biceps before sitting up. I again had my usual aroused morning condition so I tried to think about what to do with Stephen, because he probably wouldn't remember what had happened the night before. Rick slipped on his clothes and spoke in a gruff morning voice.

"I've got to go. I need to get ready for work. Have you checked on Disposable Boy?"

"No," I said. "Just go ahead. I'll take care of him."

He hugged me, gave me a kiss on the forehead, and left. I heard him go through the living room quietly to avoid waking Stephen. When I walked in the room, Stephen was still on his back, his arms thrown carelessly over his face. He slowly opened his eyes, looked around, and then looked straight at me, waiting for me to say something.

"You need to call your dad. Do it while I'm in the shower," I instructed. "Then I'll drive you wherever. I'm not going to ask you any questions, because it's not my place to know what you were up to last night. Just please have some respect for your mother and father by staying out of trouble until after her funeral."

Stephen didn't say anything but reached for the phone. I went to the shower, hoping that he would do what I told him. When I got out, he was sitting on the sofa drinking a soda. Forgetting my bathrobe, I wrapped up in a towel and he looked at me with a curiously stupid face.

"Playing hide the body?" he asked in an irritated voice.

"Whatever," I answered. "Did you call your father?"

"Yeah," he replied. "He's on his way to pick me up. I can't believe you left me sleeping on the couch. So I'm not good enough to sleep with you anymore?"

"Stephen," I raised my voice, again irritable over the whole thing, "we are no longer together, if you could ever call it that in the first place. I did you. You did me. You got used to me buying you dinner and drinks and pot. That's it. The reason why I helped you out is because there's no one else to do it. You were a good screw. It's over. Now, kindly excuse me because I'm going to be late for work."

I heard his footsteps through the house then the slam of the back door. I immediately felt bad for being such a bitch to him, given the fact that his mother was dead and I had dumped him a few nights before, but my reaction was something that couldn't be helped. In Stephen, I was looking at someone who was an intersection of death and grief, from Ayers to my own inability to be intimate, to Mrs. Clark's death, and it made me mad. I didn't want to deal with death again, even though I was going to have to, so Stephen was the scapegoat. Part of me hoped I wouldn't hear from him again, but part of me wanted to see him accomplish some sort of closure over his mother's death.

When I got to the office, my message light was already on. It was Stephen, who informed me that his mother's funeral had been set for two days later, and then he asked if I would go. I needed to go, but I didn't know how I would handle what would be the first funeral since Ayers. I sat at my desk hoping that the memories wouldn't come back. The night before, I was too busy with Stephen to think but now my mind was free again to wander. Ayers died with me by his side. He just stopped breathing after fighting for breath for nearly two days. His death was very peaceful and the pain and struggle that had been on his face for the past week were just gone, replaced by a face that was peaceful, released. The one consolation, if you could call it that, was that Ayers and I had said everything that needed to be said, so I naturally wondered if Mrs. Clark died with things on her mind. I hoped that Stephen and his brother would feel guilt over this, just like Ayers' family did. I felt a lump come up in my throat, realizing that it would be like this for a couple of days. Then another thought came to mind. I could call Rick. I found the business card he had given me and dialed his number.

"Hello, this is Rick Monette," he said cheerfully.

"Hey, it's Alex," I said.

"Hi! I was hoping you'd call. How is everything?"

"Well, Stephen is okay and the arrangements were taken care of. I need to ask you a big favor, though."

"I'll go. Don't even ask. I figure it must be pretty tough on you. I can be moral support."

"I can't believe you're willing to help me after all of this shit."

"Don't sweat it."

I could tell he was smiling just by the tone of his voice. After I hung up with Rick, my boss Madison Frehart walked into my office. Madison was the quintessential career woman, with a home and family and a solid position in a man's world. Educated at Wellesley, she decided to come back to Memphis after college in hopes of pursuing her old boyfriend, a football player from the affluent suburb where she grew up. As luck would have it, Madison didn't find the old boyfriend but instead found a former college football star who happened to be hanging out in a chic bar when she went in with a few friends. She and Peter had a whirlwind courtship and a Southern wedding to beat all Southern weddings, open bars and champagne fountains at the Peabody Hotel and a glittering dinner spread that rivaled the best state affairs. After the kids came along, Madison's persona developed even further, a powerful woman who would do anything to protect her kids but also a woman who could still hit the dance floor after a few cosmopolitans. Of course, as a powerful woman, she was drawn to gay men, and gay men to her, the allure on both sides the fashionable yet high powered straight talker who could femininely tell a cigar smoking good old boy to go fuck himself. When we started working together, we immediately became friends, and when I had the chance to work directly for her, we both agreed it was the right thing to do. Since then, business was business between us, but our personal lives were open to each other like the Sunday Lifestyle section. As we were accustomed to doing every once in a while, she plopped down with a cup of coffee for both of us and waited for me to speak. I just smiled a strange smile.

"You look guilty. Did you ..." she asked with a sly grin.

"Of course not," I said. "You know I'm not that kind of a girl. I had a rough night. Marilyn Clark died at home in her bed."

Madison froze for a moment and then relaxed a little, having known Mrs. Clark both personally and through her battery of well connected friends, neighbors, and associates.

"Was she that sick?" she asked. "That doesn't sound right. Anyway, how sad. She was quite a woman, with her charity work and such. How did Disposable Boy take it?"

"How do you think? But something else has happened," I said.

"You met someone, didn't you?" she inquired in her classically direct style.

"I did," I said, smiling, and explained to her how Rick and I had met, and that we had already been out a couple of times.

"Leave it to you, honey," she said. "All you had to do was put on your worst pair of boxers and some hottie wandered directly to your front door. I told you it wasn't going to be too late. Do you really know how hard it is to attract a man?"

I really didn't know because between Ayers, Stephen, and Rick, they just seemed to float in like snowflakes.

"So, what's he like?" she asked.

"The man is gorgeous, funny, and smart," I told her. "I almost believed he was out of my league. Now that I've been hanging out with him, I'm starting to feel weird. His knock on the door gives me butterflies. I check the mirror before I open it."

"You've been given a great gift," she said, waxing wise much like the therapist she had become. "Even though you may not see it that way. Ayers' death gave you the start of the journey to your true self. Sure, you were in love with him and he with you, and you were on the same wavelength. Now that you've had to go it alone, you've really discovered who you are and what you want out of life."

As she was saying this, I thought about the almost-perfect life Ayers and I had together, but I also thought of its imperfections. He was moody, while I was impatient and childlike. I was also totally dependent on him because I couldn't change a tire or unclog the dryer vent, but on the other hand, he couldn't balance a checkbook worth a damn. He and I probably would have been together forever, but that was not meant to be. So many times I abused him with my temper, throwing things and screaming obscenities at the top of my lungs. In one particularly vocal incident, Ayers looked right at me and yelled back, "What, do you want to hit me? Go ahead and take your best shot but you're fucking crazy if you think I would ever raise a hand to you!"

I saw that the gift Madison was talking about was the fact that life made two decisions for me. First, life decided to make a strong-willed, six-foot, 200-pound muscle boy completely dependent on me. When Ayers became ill, he couldn't bathe, dress, or even piss without assistance. I didn't want anyone else to help him, so I was there the entire time. I wasn't about to let his mother or his sister see him in that condition. Second, life decided to take him away just after we had become the closest in our relationship. I was brought to my knees and forced to make changes.

"Death makes us examine our own lives," said Madison, speaking from experience. "Remember when I told you how I took care of my grandfather when he was sick with lung cancer? When he died I knew immediately how frail life really is, and how much of a gift each second on earth really is. You've been given the same knowledge, love."

Madison had come from a background that was much like mine, a proper Southern religious background. She became very self-reliant when she took care of her sick grandfather over a summer during college, the man she credited with opening her mind more than her family had ever allowed it to be opened. Madison's grandfather had been a professor at a small liberal arts college in Missouri, an unlikely place for a forward thinking faculty, so when he got sick she looked at it as the opportunity of a lifetime. When she went back to school, her entire outlook on life had changed, so she sought out the company of the people she had shunned before, the minorities, the strong women, and the gay men. On her first date with Peter, Madison flat out told him that if he didn't like black or gay people that she was not the woman for him, that her friends were a package deal. She could always hit the nail on the head, or "pin the wig on the drag queen" as she usually put it. We had a joke that she was never wrong, and I really don't think she ever proved that joke incorrect.

"Your soul needs some freedom," she said, "so give up the things that are binding you and you'll be truly free to love and live again."

I nodded blankly in agreement with her.

"Take time to be still and listen to your inner voice," she instructed, "and you'll realize that profound silence provides the best direction you can take."

I took most of this seriously but had to break the mood.

"If we were on the beach, this could be a douche commercial," I said.

Madison responded in her best gay man's voice. "Now girl, don't you do me like that!"

I always looked up to her because she was a person who had found a comfortable spirituality and was not afraid to talk to people about it, in a world where many spiritual people knew nothing more than quoting the Bible and telling you that Jesus would save you if you would repent from all of your evil ways. When it came to therapy, I got more from a morning conversation with Madison than I did from an expensive shrink whose clients were paying for his beach house in Destin. She was right, since my decision to end things with Stephen had come from my inner voice. I was finally heading in the right direction.

CHAPTER 9

▼

SOMETIMES IT'S JUST THE DRAMA VALUE

The day of Marilyn Clark's funeral was cooler and clearer than it had been all summer, although "cooler" in Southern summers meant ninety degrees and ninety percent humidity, as opposed to one hundred degrees and one hundred percent humidity. I dramatically took the day off, going against my own admonitions that gays give out sympathy for the same reason. Rick called around eight and I invited him over for coffee. Our evenings had been spent together, talking, laughing, and discussing life. I was so attracted to Rick that it was hard for me not to hit on him every time he was around. He showed up wearing linen drawstring pants and a tight white t-shirt, so we could both sense the tension and we both enjoyed it.

How can he think of enticing me at a time like this? I thought dramatically.

He sipped his coffee with those suckable lips. We really didn't talk very much. It was one of those times where we could tell that silence was going to be golden. Rick put his arm around me, remaining quiet, and the only words that passed between us were when he was going to come pick me up.

We drove to the church in silence, his hand resting on my shoulder the entire time, as if he wanted me to know that he was there for me. When we got to the church, it was very crowded. I knew Mrs. Clark had been popular in social circles but the diversity of the people in attendance surprised me, from the conservative ladies of the daughters of some all white establishment that maliciously still existed to the local chapter of the gay Democrats. We walked down the aisle toward the front, where the silver casket waited, covered with a spray of red roses and a beautiful photo of Mrs. Clark.

"I can see," Rick whispered, "where Stephen got his looks."

Stephen, his father, his brother, and the young Mrs. Clark were in the first pew, looking very uncomfortable. We sat down diagonally from them and Stephen turned to glance at me, looking like someone had hit him in both eyes, his look for the day a combination of grief, drugs, and lack of sleep. Young Mrs. Clark smiled and nodded, and then Stephen started to cry. I mouthed "hi" and looked away, but I noticed that a blonde, blue-eyed, very tan, and extremely well built stranger was sitting near the family.

I went through a three year dry spell and now the hotties are everywhere, I thought.

The stranger's blonde hair fell in strands over his forehead, giving him a forlorn yet sexy look, like the overdrawn Tom of Finland characters that were famous for having sex anywhere and everywhere. When Rick looked over in that direction, he raised his eyebrows very discreetly, in a gesture that he apparently thought would be undetectable to everyone but me. The sight of a grieving family, a casket, and the sweet smell of flowers were all too familiar. I couldn't help wandering back in my mind to the day of Ayers' funeral when I sat in the front row with my head in my hands, breaking my mother's rule, crying so hard that the tears started to drop on the floor, on my knees, and run down my sleeves, and no one could comfort me. Before that, I walked at the head of the family behind the casket as it was brought into the church. I walked and cried, walked and cried my way down the aisle very dramatically, but for once, I was not aware of the drama value of what was going on. I remember glancing at one of my friends, a friend who never showed emotion, sobbing, as he watched me take that lonely walk.

I was startled to hear the priest begin intoning the service for Mrs. Clark, but I couldn't concentrate on his words. I felt as if the world was shimmering around me, like looking up through clear yet deep water, except in reds and blues. I let out an agonizing sigh and Rick reached over and put his hand on my leg. The service ended before I could think again, but I ended up pretty numb from the experience and Rick could tell. The family mourned their way back up the aisle behind Mrs. Clark's casket, and as we all stood to go the cars, I handed the keys to Rick quietly and without ceremony. He held my hand tightly for a few seconds before taking them. I was hoping that Stephen's family would get into the limo before I got out there, because I did not feel like talking to anyone anymore.

As the procession moved through the streets I felt it all again. I traveled in the funeral home's limo behind the hearse, along with Ayers' family, suffering through the loneliest feeling I've ever had, surrounded by people, yet a million miles away from them. I couldn't look out the windows because everything reminded me of Ayers, and I couldn't look forward because the hearse was always right there. All of these feelings were rushing back so quickly that I had to do something, so I looked at Rick as the tears tried to come out. He looked bewildered, as if he wanted to say something but just couldn't.

At the cemetery, the crowd gathered as the casket was carried from the hearse to the gravesite. The family and a few people were able to sit under the tent while the rest of the crowd swelled around, standing. The blonde stranger stood near Stephen, which made me think that this could be Stephen's latest acquisition, a quick rebound. The priest said a few more words that I didn't hear and really didn't want to hear. When it was done, Stephen, his brother, and their father laid red roses on the top of the casket, something that was eerily exact to what we did for Ayers. After his funeral I stood next to his casket longer than necessary, holding the rose in my hand, the tears dripping down onto the cold metal. When Mrs. Clark's crowd began to disperse, I left Rick for a moment to find Stephen. Unusual circumstances could sometimes make us feel things that we really didn't, but I felt something for Stephen. I couldn't figure out what it was, a feeling that was telling me to clear the air between us and let him know that I was there if he needed someone to talk to. He seemed so alone there, even with all of the people milling around and waiting to talk to him, even among his own family members. When I caught his eye, I motioned for him to come over. He excused himself politely from the daughters of the Old South, some of them looking like they had actually been present when Lee surrendered, and came over to where I was standing. His blonde friend was watching the whole thing while speaking to Rick with very strained expressions and body language, as if he wanted to gesture wildly and open his mouth instead of speaking through gritted teeth.

"Hi," I said to Stephen.

"Hullo," he said sullenly. "Thanks for coming."

"Look," I said, "I wanted to apologize for being so harsh with you the other day. You know we can't go on like we were before, but I want you to know that I'm here if you need someone to talk to."

Stephen's eyes brightened. "Really?" he asked. "It sounded like you wanted to be done with me, dude. Anyway, I'm trying to move on."

"I'm here," I said, "as a friend. You don't have to move on from that if you don't want to."

Stephen looked over to his blonde friend, who was now standing alone, and gave a little smirk. Between the two of them, there was way too much irreverence for a cemetery so I walked away.

I turned to Rick and said simply, "let's go now."

CHAPTER 10

▼

ARE YOU READY FOR THIS?

A few days later I felt like things were becoming normal again. My work was keeping me mercifully busy and Rick and I were together often. I enjoyed spending time with him because we clicked so entirely in such a short time that we naturally wanted to be together whenever we could. I kept thinking that we were finishing each other's sentences and had not even had sex yet, a choice that I wasn't sure if we were consciously making or not. I was hoping that it would all happen when the time was right, and I was proud of my ability to resist the temptation to jump into bed. He assured me that we were doing the right thing and I usually felt that way until we kissed goodnight, but after that I wanted him each time.

About two weeks after Mrs. Clark's funeral, Rick and I went out for dinner and drinks on a Friday night. The normal crowd was present at our usual spot, or as near to normal as our neighborhood bunch could be on a Friday night, so it wasn't very long before we saw Stephen come in and take a place at the bar. We watched him with interest while he waited on the Goldilocks Gang, as Rick referred to his posse of grunge boys. When they showed up, all of them ordered drinks and I watched in amazement as Stephen paid the bill. Rick looked over at me as if he knew what I was thinking and started laughing, his eyes flashing with a mischievous glint. Stephen looked over and saw us, and I nearly dropped my cocktail when Rick waved him over.

"Good God," I said. "What in hell are you doing?"

"Like any good nosy neighbor," Rick replied, "I'm trying to figure out what a penniless drug addict is doing buying a round of drinks in this place. Enjoy it."

After he said this, Rick winked at me and I went wobbly.

Stephen sauntered over, gave us each a quick hug, and plopped himself down at our table. Rick shot a quick glance at me and opened his mouth to speak. I looked down, hoping to stifle the laughter I was about to spit out.

"What's up man?" Rick growled. "You buying drinks for your boys, big spender? You are apparently on the road to dealing with grief."

"Well, dudes," Stephen started speaking slowly, using that word again. "Mom left me everything that was hers. I got the house, the car, and most of the money. I also administer my brother's inheritance. See, Mom had some money of her own and then when Dad left she took him to the cleaners. I guess I can sit back and relax for a while, you know, figure out what I want to do."

Rick and I stared at him for more than a polite second, being too stunned to reply.

A few days after his mother's funeral, Stephen explained he'd received a call from her attorney, an invitation to come to his office downtown to talk about his mother's estate. Stephen had never heard anyone in his family refer to an estate, so he wasn't sure if the invitation was good or bad. When he mentioned the lawyer's summons to his brother, Andrew told him that he had heard nothing about it, and insisted that there were probably going to be problems related to her will because of her divorce from their father. When Stephen arrived at the law office, he was ushered in right away, seated at a conference table, and offered biscotti and cappuccino. He vaguely knew the attorney and put on his best businesslike face, just as they taught him at Ole Miss. His mother, the attorney explained, addressing him as "Mr. Clark" and calling him "Sir", had invested both her divorce settlement and her own money well, and had left a liquid estate valued somewhere around a million dollars. Of course, the house and the Benz S500 would go to Stephen to dispose of as he wished, although a sale of the house would require the attorney's assistance. The attorney hoped that Stephen would take his time to decide, and perhaps he would like to move into the house while he made his decision. When Stephen asked about his brother, the attorney told him that he was appointed by his mother to administer his brother's inheritance. As Stephen explained this to us, I knew that it was still too much for him.

"Anyway," Stephen said as he once again looked over at Rick. "I'm having a party at the house next Saturday night and I really want you two to come. I'm having it catered and everything. It'll be really nice. Anyway, gotta go."

Stephen got up and walked away. I stared at my glass while Rick tossed back the last of his martini, then popped the olive in his mouth and said "Well my my," in his best Southern Belle voice. He reached over and lifted my face up with his index finger, still smiling and chomping that olive.

"Stop taking that kid's troubles on your shoulders," he said softly. "Obviously his mother didn't know and his father doesn't really care. After all, she took him to the cleaners, didn't she? Just like her best Dior frock."

Rick spoke again. "I guess you must've contemplated death since Ayers. I suppose I have, too. Sometimes I wonder if we're rewarded for all the stuff we go through in life."

I thought about death every day since Ayers died, gnawing on it in a different way every time. A few days after his death there was a terrible train derailment somewhere out West. Several people died, among them a few teenagers, most of them drowning when the railcars went off a bridge and into a swamp. I wondered childishly the night of the train accident if the afterlife had a Welcome Center, where new members helped other new members get used to being dead. I remember thinking that Ayers' wonderfully sweet personality would have been perfect to be a greeter on the other side, to help people deal with the reality of having died. I also began reading books about people who had death experiences and people who claimed to be able to travel to the other dimensions at will, a desperate attempt to find some common ground between Ayers and me. Then, after a few months I got mad at nature for taking someone away from me, someone who had not had the chance to live his life yet. I had trouble believing that any supreme being could let bad things happen to people who would not hurt a fly, despite my religious upbringing. It became harder and harder to talk to anyone in my family because their comfort was always tinged with some sort of religious belief or Bible quotes, something that I was sure worked when all was well but could malfunction at the point of despair. The shrinks told me over and over again that what I was feeling was normal, but no one had the answer on how to get past it. It was all a consolation of the fact that time would heal my grief.

Sitting at the table with Rick that night, all my feelings leading up to that moment became clear. I was afraid something bad would happen to a good relationship since I had already lived that situation. To add to my mixed-up feelings, I became a major hypochondriac after Ayers died, having watched a healthy person turn deathly sick in the space of six months. Every pimple made me think I had skin cancer, while a headache did not send me to find the Advil but would send me into a fit of fear that I had developed a brain tumor. My friends and family put it off to the drama thing again, but there were a few nights where I couldn't fall asleep for fear that I wasn't going to wake up the next day. My anger, pitted with the all-out hypochondria, turned me into a pessimistic person who did not believe that life could ever come into balance between all of its elements, health, love, family, and career. Whenever I heard of someone's success, the little scary man in the back of my head would say something like, "don't brag too much or you'll get the flesh-eating bacteria and die". I became angry with people who seemed to have the balance between their elements without a piano falling on their heads or suddenly dying from being bitten by a rogue malaria-carrying mosquito. Time had indeed softened my grief and my anger, but I still wondered about the possibility of ever achieving some sort of comfortable balance.

"I wonder," I said, "if life is ever like we really want it? Are things ever in harmony or in a perfect arrangement? Some people seem to have perfect arrangement in their lives, you know?"

"Ah," Rick interjected, "things appear to be perfect. They may be perfect on the outside but what about the inside? I know what would make life perfect."

He smiled as he said that. I looked up with a puzzled look, not sure what he had said.

"You," he sweetly answered, then added quickly, "naked, with just enough chocolate pudding to cover the good parts."

I sat there in stunned silence as he smiled again, excused himself, and headed for the restroom. I couldn't believe that this guy wanted me. The waitress, who was normally there when we were, came back by the table to check on us. "If it seems too good to be true honey," she said, one hand on her hip, "it probably is. You better find out, he may like to roll around naked in chocolate pudding or something."

I laughed at this uncanny comment as the waitress put her hand on my shoulder and winked at me. I looked over toward the bar and saw Rick talking to Stephen's group. Actually, he was talking to the blond guy who was suddenly with Stephen, the same guy from the funeral. I watched with amusement and curiosity, but without jealousy, which surprised me. Rick looked up and smiled at me, the smile that could melt a polar ice cap. When Rick came back over, I started up an entirely different conversation.

"Who's the stud?" I inquired. "You apparently know him."

"It's a long story," Rick answered. "And I'll tell you at some point but let's just say we know each other from Atlanta."

I knew that Blondie and Rick had a connection, and I believed that the connection was intimate, but how strange that I felt completely at peace with all of this. Rick had a calming influence on me; something I'd desperately needed for quite some time, so the peace I felt was not really a stretch.

Rick sighed, took a sip of his martini then spoke. "Alex, I've had time to reflect. I've had time to figure out what I want. My career doesn't make my life. My car doesn't make my life. My house doesn't make my life. Being happy just being me and learning about my true self is the key to happiness. The right someone special in my life would be the ultimate icing on the cake. You're everything I have ever wanted. You're intelligent, cute, funny, spiritual, and not afraid to be yourself. I just hope you can deal with me."

My fear had always been that my baggage would be too much, that a potential love match would look at my history and politely decline. I would sometimes break it down in my own head, the pro and con list of dating Alex Palini, the top pros being a successful career, a decent sense of humor, and a nice butt, while the cons tended to go with the grieving anger and the hypochondria. How, I reasoned, would anybody want to deal with a guy who was mad at the world for taking away his first love and who automatically assumed that a simple cold was going to end up as a bird flu fatality?

"Deal with you?" I asked loudly. "How can you be so sure you can deal with me?"

"I don't know," he replied, "but it feels right. For all I know you could be a dud in bed, although from what I can tell you're not. But that doesn't matter to me anymore. It's love and companionship that matter. You have to be friends to be lovers and physical love and attraction falls into place when the spiritual and emotional sides are together. I feel like I know you so well … shit, we may have been lovers in some past life."

"Elizabeth and Lord Robert?" I said, to lighten the mood.

"Hmmm, Bonnie and Clyde."

"Cleo and Marc?"

"Tammy and George."

"Let's go, Tammy," I said back to him, placing my hand on top of his.

When we got back to my apartment, I kissed him and sent him on his way. I didn't want to be alone but I needed to be. I really didn't know if I was ready for this.

CHAPTER 11

▼

WORKING UP TO IT

On Monday I went to the office early, but Madison was already there. Calling out to her as I sat down at my desk, I looked at the pile of work left from Friday. Madison appeared in the doorway, dressed as usual to the nines, wearing a perfectly cut black Chanel suit and runway-hot Prada shoes that I helped pick out on a lunchtime shopping run. She stood in the doorway of my office with two cups of coffee in her hand, then walked over and sat at one of the chairs at my conference table.

"You know," she said, settling in for a chat, "it seems strange to me that a boss would actually bring coffee to her employee. It should be the other way around but, since I'm so wonderful and fabulous, I do these things for you."

"Whatever," I replied. "What brings you in so early?"

"What do you think? The Hernandez account. It seems to take up most of my time," she sighed as she looked over her cup. "But you never come in this early. You can't sleep because you're falling for him and you don't want to. It's time to let go, Alex."

"I know," I replied. "But it's like this wall has gone up. Rick makes me fall all over myself but I'm so afraid of being hurt. It's like losing your sight. You know how things are supposed to look and would give anything to see them again."

"You still haven't slept with him, have you?" asked Madison.

"What's that got to do with it?" I raised my voice. "If anything it shows that I'm taking things slowly."

"You are, Dearest," she said, sounding like my mother. "Still, you have to let go of your real issue before you can enjoy a physical relationship with him. You know, Disposable Boy fulfilled the physical need but couldn't fulfill the other need. Maybe Rick can do both. I still want to meet him. Don't go too slow though, because you know you queens act faster than an Ex-Lax brownie."

Our administrative assistant Jen came in at that moment, carrying an open box of long-stemmed red roses from Gilroy's. It was normally Madison who got flowers from Peter, so she stood up, smoothed out her skirt, and smiled while Jen began to laugh.

"Sorry Madison," she said. "These are for hot pants over here." She motioned in my direction.

Although I was surprised, I still managed to reply, "Ever heard of sexual harassment?"

I did my best Bette Davis walk past Jen and pulled the card from the box, which she placed on my credenza. I stared at the card and managed a great big smile as I read the silly words written by Rick himself:

> *Just a quick note to say*
> *Have a perfectly arranged day*
> *Can't wait to see you.*
> *Tammy*

I sank into my chair while my ears burned. Madison and Jen were smiling, standing over me like a couple of vultures waiting for the road kill to finally croak. I could not believe that this guy wanted to be with me like this, then I realized that the thought of him sending me flowers turned me on. Looking at my crotch, I quickly scooted up under my desk and glanced at Madison.

"So," I said in my most professional voice, "what *is* the problem with the Hernandez account, anyway?"

Madison reached down and snatched the card from my desk. She also looked with amusement at my feeble attempt to hide my hard-on.

"Nice try, Alex," she said, wagging her manicured finger. "You forget I live with three boys."

I simply sat there, staring dumbly and sipping coffee.

"I'm an expert on penises," she said coldly, causing me to choke over my coffee. "So I know what's going on. This guy turns you on in every way, and, judging from these words, he's ready to register at Home Depot already, and you're ready to let him." Madison winked at me, got up, and was back to business. "I've got a conference call. Lunch at Margo's? I'm craving their mushroom tortellini."

Without looking up from my work, I smiled and then answered her. "Whatever. We'll talk later, huh?"

My phone rang and I was immediately thrown into the business of the day, although my thoughts once again returned to a day when Ayers sent flowers to the office. He did not call to make sure I got them, but dropped in instead. The only person in the office who knew who he was at the time was Madison, who smiled knowingly and let things happen. Ayers turned to lock my office door and turned back to me, smiling. When he left, he gave Madison a sly wink.

I managed to get some work done before she came to my door saying how hungry she was. We left the office headed back to Margo's, the place with the gayest name and the gayest clientele. Madison equated getting a Brazilian wax with having lunch in straight hangouts, insisting that lunchtime was when she needed to stimulate her mind after complex work at the office.

When we arrived at Margo's the usual lunch crowd was there. We got a table near the middle of the place, where we could see everything and everyone. I spoke to the "usual suspects", as Madison referred to my neighborhood friends who also lunched there at least once a week. As we were enjoying our lunch, Madison glanced toward the door and kicked me under the table, a sure sign that she had seen someone we knew. I looked toward the door and saw Stephen with Blondie, Rick's weird connection. Stephen made eye contact with Madison, and then he and Blondie came over to the table. Madison had been introduced to Stephen during our pseudo-relationship, at a point when I was proud to be dating such a young and attractive guy. When Madison first met him, she lowered her Chanel sunglasses down her nose to peer over them.

"Hel-*lo*," she had said, and then pursed her lips with a pout.

I do remember that we had lunch together on various occasions, Madison playing the flirt with Stephen who soaked it up like a sponge. Stephen was always on his best behavior around her, a motive I questioned until I found out that she had worked with Mrs. Clark on a charity event.

"Hi Alex," he said hoarsely. "How are you? Hello, Madison. I'd like you guys to meet Nick Bannister. He's from Atlanta."

Nick shook our hands and pleasantly greeted us, although he eyed me strangely. Stephen seemed to be using Nick as a trophy, showing him off, a sadly ironic coincidence to my use of Stephen. He met Nick on Manlink, the website that allowed horny men to go straight to the sex without having to buy drinks or flirt in person. I discovered this much later, about the time I discovered that the two met on the website while I was still with Stephen, another annoyance that Stephen didn't think anything of. When it came to Manlink, even the respectable among us used the service when we wanted company but didn't want to go the traditional route. After I met Stephen, I retired my account, thinking that at least I could settle into a routine with the same guy. Stephen maintained an innocent correspondence with Nick for a few months, although Nick's x-rated pictures on the website caused Stephen to flirt incessantly while talking about his older boyfriend. After all, what could become of a cyber-sex relationship with a guy in Atlanta?

After I dumped Stephen on that smoky night in my bedroom, he trashed me to Nick who decided to be the white knight, riding in from Atlanta to rescue the poor, now-single Stephen, who had been dumped for this Rick-what's-his-name, the florist guy from Atlanta. The two hooked up at one of the local bars, and after one drink headed back to Nick's hotel room at the French Quarter Inn, where the heart-shaped Jacuzzi tub in room 214 was never the same again. Nick, quite the visionary, decided that he could use Stephen to get to Rick and to me, but ended up developing feelings for Stephen, who suspected nothing. By the time Madison and I saw them that day, Stephen and Nick were together constantly but had not been exposed to the seedier sides of each other's personalities. Stephen also quit his job, counting on using his mother's money until something better came along.

"So," said Stephen, "I'm having a party Saturday night at my house, around nine. You're both invited. Bring a date. By the way, I quit my job. See ya."

He really didn't give us much of a chance to say yes or no, and since he had already invited Rick and me I wasn't about to say anything. Madison and I watched them as they walked away, and I wondered why Stephen would invite Madison to what promised to be a freak-fest at his inherited house. Then I processed what he had said right before he and Nick walked away.

"Did he say 'quit my job'?" I asked.

"I believe those were his exact words, Honey," she replied.

"I wouldn't mind sneaking up behind that in the shower," she added, indicating Nick. "But, as usual, the best looking ones are playing for your team. You know, I may go to that party to see what's going on. I also want to see the inside of that house. Marilyn Clark was known for her taste."

"Are you serious?" I inquired. "Would you really go? Maybe you can come over early and have a cocktail with Rick."

"Sure," said Madison "I can't wait. My inner queen bee is telling me that things aren't exactly as they seem."

"Why did the little shit quit his job?" I asked, fixated on the need to make a living.

"Why work at his age if he can live off his mother's money?" Madison asked seriously. "Wouldn't you have done the same thing those many, many, many years before when you were twenty-something?"

"Maybe," I said. "Hey, I think there were a couple of extra many's in there. I guess if I got three you'd get four."

"Don't forget," Madison replied with her know-it-all smile, "I can wreck your next bonus, buddy boy!"

When I got back to the office, Rick had called. When I returned the call, he seemed overjoyed that I'd called him back. I asked him out for dinner and we agreed to meet at my apartment at seven for drinks and dinner at The Terrace, a place for a great dinner and romantic atmosphere. Rick told me that he really wanted to talk, and I could not imagine what it was about, although the no fear attitude I adopted after Ayers' death told me nothing could shock me anymore.

CHAPTER 12

▼

PERFECT ARRANGEMENT?

I stood in the shower soaking my back because the gym was again full of younger guys, flexing their muscles and strutting about. I still looked at them, these hot guys and their hard bodies, and I always hoped they still looked at me, too. So, this particular day, the day of my dinner date with Rick, my back was strained not from the workout but from looking around too much *while* I was working out. Was I really ready for another relationship or did I want to have a no strings attached relationship, the kind where sex happens and I would be guaranteed a date for Saturday nights? My mind and other body parts told me that I wanted to have steamy sex with no intimate attachment, but since Rick came into the picture, one of those inner voices I had not heard in a long time told me I was wrong.

After getting dressed, I stood in front of the mirror. I'd chosen a dark blue Theory shirt that flattered my chest, along with flat front khakis, and then I sluttily left two buttons undone on the bottom of the shirt to expose my stomach and my silver belt buckle.

"Pretty good," I said to my reflection. "I hope Rick gets a kick out of it."

The phone rang at that moment, and I expected it to be Rick telling me he was late.

"Hello?" I said in my best sexy hoarse voice.

"Uh, Doreen," said the voice on the other end, "could you step over here for a minute?"

Immediately, I recognized the voice of one of my closest friends Stuart McGuire, my own personal shrink, drag queen, and Joan Rivers all wrapped into one big package.

"Feathers!" I shouted into the phone, using the name Stuart had given himself. "I haven't heard from you in ages."

It had only been a few days since I last heard from Stuart, but the drama value of "ages" played well with him. I knew Stuart from as far back as college, when I worked part time in an investment firm where he was a management trainee. It was a casual relationship because more than anything I was afraid of him, the loud, painfully direct guy with no fear. We didn't see each other for about two years after I graduated, because I went to work in a bank and Stuart worked his way up in the investment firm. When I had finally had enough of the banking business and its old ladies who would withdraw hundreds of thousands of dollars over a tiny percentage point of interest, I quit, the first time in my life I did not have a plan to go forward. Jobless, I went out every night with a group of similarly equipped people, dancing, drinking, smoking pot, and having gropey but-not-all-the-way sex in back rooms until six in the morning and scheduling interviews in the afternoons. Since Stuart was working hard and I was playing, we rarely ran into each other until a spring night when I was outside of the club smoking a cigarette with my loser friends. I casually approached Stuart, who let his real personality loose on me at that point.

"Alex, you stud!" he yelled over the crowd. "You are so fucking hot!"

With a reintroduction like that, I couldn't ignore him, so I started talking to him about the nothing I called my life. After a few minutes, the conversation turned serious when he told me that the firm was in great need of new investment reps, and didn't I have my licensing? He told me that Madison was also in the management training program and that they were both ready to be promoted. I had the job in two weeks, with Stuart to thank for it.

Our work relationship took on more of the tone of the bar conversation, putting on serious faces during meetings with management or with clients. The three of us took lunch together, went out for drinks together, and founded a friendship that was built on more than our work. Stuart prided himself on being able to "read the book" to anyone who displeased him, either to their face or privately when the three of us were in a conference room together. He even wrote what he called "The Book", a collection of ways to start an "I've had it with you" conversation, which I still kept on my office desk. The thing about Stuart was that when he read "The Book", to me or anyone else, nine out of ten times he was right, a rare quality in such a judgmental person. Stuart changed my life in many ways and was there for me when things were really bad. At some point in my deliberation over whether to take up with Stephen or not, Stuart became very angry, accusing me of taking for granted that I was still young, pretty, and muscular, and that someone younger, prettier, and leaner had a serious, although sexual, interest in me. He told me it was stupid to deliberate and prudent to jump in and get my rocks off and to get on with my "fucking life". In fact, a few days before that reading of "The Book", Stuart decided to try to hit on Stephen himself, doing his usual flaunt of the money and promises of a larger than life sexual experience. As disgusting as it seemed later, I watched from a distance as Disposable Boy turned him down. If Stuart liked you, a reading of "The Book" was immediately followed by business as usual, so my friendship with him was a part of my life, something I had come to rely on, and the best source of good natured and constant jealousy. When he left the firm, his next career move was perfect.

As a management consultant, he traveled several days a week, getting paid a zillion dollars an hour to tell people what was wrong with their business, the perfect job for a person like Stuart McGuire. I had managed over the past month to keep my mouth shut about Rick, so the only thing I told Stuart was that I had been seeing someone and used all of our busy schedules as an excuse. I did tell him that Rick was running Gilroy's, just for the value of hearing him gush over my new florist boyfriend.

"Honey," cooed Stuart, "Disposable Boy asked me to go to a party at his house on Saturday. Is this going to be one of those junior romper-room things where I can get a load of all those young-uns?"

Stuart's biggest goal in life at the time was to attract younger guys like Stephen, who had no other interest than money and sex with an older yet good looking "tall-n-natural" redhead. Stuart was currently between flings and I often wondered if he would ever settle down for real. An invitation from Stephen was a good chance for him to find another twenty-something boy toy. The last fling told me in great detail about the beauty of their sex life, so Stuart not only spoiled a guy materially but sexually as well. His men, if you could call them that, were usually a couple of steps below Stephen in their tact and deportment, so I routinely shut my ears when the boy toy mentioned a designer shirt with buttons, Diesel underwear, and any kind of alcoholic drinks in between.

"Of course," I snapped. "Have you talked to Madison?"

If Madison were really going to this ridiculous party, Stuart would be tacked onto her like a game of pin-the-wig-on-the-drag-queen.

"Is Brad Pitt doable?" smarted Stuart. "I'll be coming over for cocktails with Madison, so I can meet this new man of yours and judge him early."

"Sounds great," I replied. "Now will you let me go? Rick is going to be here any minute."

"Oh, a booty-call, huh?" asked Stuart. "Make sure your coochie is clean."

"For your information," I said, "*we* have not actually done anything except kiss. I *know* it's hard for you to believe that two men can actually date and not have sex, but it's true."

I was rather pleased with myself for this comment, keeping in mind that the pretend animosity between Stuart and I was a source of humor for all.

"Whatevah!" retorted Stuart. "You go and finish beating your wig. I'll call you Saturday."

Stuart finished the conversation with his flight attendant, "Bye-bye now," and I was left with a smile on my face, knowing for sure that he would eat his heart out over Rick. I checked the mirror one last time and went into the living room to mix drinks. A moment later, Rick knocked on my front door, and when I opened it, I saw my Adonis again, smiling brightly, leaning on the doorway, wearing a starched white shirt and black pants.

How does he manage to dress like that and not look like the caterer? I thought, smiling.

He stepped inside and kissed me on the cheek, but I still had trouble speaking around him. I could tell he was for some reason deep in thought, so I just acted as the perfect host, serving cosmopolitans that were actually red this time instead of light pink. The drive to the restaurant was quiet, punctuated by the sounds of the city through the open roof and Nancy Wilson singing about her gentleman friend. Although Rick was quiet, he smiled, held my hand, and let the silence speak for itself. I knew he wanted to talk, but I couldn't quite decide why. I assumed it was because he wanted to explain his connection with Nick, but once again, I believed that nothing could shock me.

I made a reservation for a small quiet table in a corner near a window, with not much traffic from the kitchen or the restrooms, with a good server who was not overly attentive, a guarantee of privacy. I ordered a bottle of Chilean red wine, the kind that is smooth enough to sneak up on you. We talked about our day at work. I told him about Stuart, and I told him that we were all anxious to go to Stephen's party for different reasons. Then it happened.

"Alex," said Rick quietly. "Let's talk."

He reached over the table and took my hand, which made me feel like my engagement ring was going to be hiding in a soufflé at the dinner table.

"Sure," I replied calmly, wanting to scream.

"Alex," he said, "I really like you, a lot. I haven't had feelings like this in a long time. We have such a great time together. You're cute, funny, and you do have a great little body. I know I could fall for you, but I haven't let myself."

All I could do was nod stupidly because I had no idea where this was going.

"The reason I haven't let myself go," Rick continued, "is that I've gotten used to being hurt. Let's just say I haven't had much luck at love. First, you should know that Nick, Stephen's latest screw, is actually my ex. We were together for a few years, a few years too many."

Rick waited to see if there was any reaction. I really did not have a reaction to this news because it really wasn't that hard to figure out. I wondered if Nick was always this scuzzy acting, but I didn't want to ask.

"Was he always that scuzzy acting?" I blurted, the Chilean wine already sneaking up on me.

Rick laughed.

"No," he answered, although unconvincingly. "He was really a gentleman for a long time. He used to keep himself up better, too. I'll have to show you a picture."

"Okay," I spoke up again, getting bolder by the minute, "what happened and why the hell is he here?"

I could not believe the way that came out, but I went with it anyway.

"Well," he replied, "I really don't know. I spoke to him briefly after Mrs. Clark's funeral while you were talking to someone else. He wanted to see me but I told him no."

I began to wonder what was up.

"Okay," Rick interrupted my thoughts, "well …"

He stopped again, which was very unusual for him, then continued, haltingly. My mind started to worry over the possibilities of this conversation.

"See Alex, I … um, well," He stumbled over his words, and then took a ragged breath. "I'm about to put a major deal-breaker out there. I'm HIV positive."

When he said it, I felt my face turn hot. The motions of the restaurant seemed to slow into moving globs of color while I heard voices from all around me but felt completely disconnected from them. Then everything began to speed up, rushing around me like a flash flood of color and sound. I looked back at Rick who was just sitting there with his eyebrows raised. A spin started, the world being tossed around in front of me like I was on a corkscrew roller coaster, something my Southern relatives would have called "the vapors", then it all stopped.

I looked at Rick again, fighting my own disbelief. I was not uneducated about HIV, I knew that medical advancements had changed the way we looked at people living with it. To look at Rick, you would never know he had it. The man was gorgeous, muscular, and could run ten miles a day, six days a week. Then it hit me, the issue that kept me from stepping right through this latest wrinkle, the thing that really could be the deal-breaker. Could I risk losing someone again? What if he left me like Ayers did? What if I ended up with two dead husbands instead of one? Could I face watching someone I loved become a total burden, with no way to take care of himself again? Rick broke the silence.

"Baby," he said, almost crying, "I want to be with you. I want to have a relationship with you. You're the best. But you have to decide if it's worth it."

At some point, one of the rushing colors and sounds was the server bringing our food. I stared down at the plate, hungry but unwilling to eat. Rick had actually started to eat, so I started to ask a question.

"How ..." I began, but stopped.

"I've been living with this for six years," he answered, as if he were reading my mind, "and it happened because I made one irresponsible choice, one time. I got carried away. It just happened. We were drunk and it just happened. I know that I may have to pay for this mistake."

"Was it Nick?" I asked trivially, as if knowing where it came from could make a difference.

"No," he answered, looking down at his food. "It was just a guy I knew."

My mind took over again. He was healthy. He could live with it for a long time if he took care of himself. But the pain I had been through with Ayers was something I never wanted to feel again. I could love this man, but was it worth that pain? I remembered the blackness I felt inside after Ayers died, that empty feeling nothing could fill, the spirit-breaking disappointment of dreaming about him and then waking up and feeling his side of the bed, only to snap back to the reality of the fact that he wasn't there. I remembered the feeling of grief as a huge wall, a metal wall that I couldn't go around, through, or over. The wall just hung there for so long, blocking the sunlight and keeping me in this perpetual twilight of grief, not quite darkness because I did have the memories of him but not quite light because he wasn't coming back. My rational side answered my own questions by injecting thoughts like someone would inject a needle: you could get splattered across the road by a bus, you could get sucked up by a tornado, or you could hook up with a mad drape-strangler. Why put a timeline on it?

"God," I said, looking into Rick's gorgeous eyes. "I don't know what to say. I do know that my mind is working a mile a minute, so I'm not ready to say no."

"See," Rick said, "Nick left me because he just couldn't handle it. It's like he couldn't handle the suspense or something. I have to go to the doctor every six months. I'm an exercise fanatic. I'm not about to let this beat me. Look, Alex, we're both strong people. I deal with this every day and you've dealt with death in an intimate way. I need you to think about it. I want you to fall in love with me."

I did not eat much for dinner and the silence in the car on the ride home was a strange one, not an angry silence or a silence of denial but a genuine silence that could not be broken. When we got back, I told Rick that I needed some time to think about things.

"How long?" he inquired.

"As long as it takes," I answered.

I went up to my apartment alone and tried to go through the motions of getting ready for bed. It was about eleven o'clock but I could not fall asleep. My first thoughts were of Ayers. I had known deep down, that he was not going to make it, but he stayed so optimistic, even when the shit came back.

"They say," he stated, "that I can take more chemo and pretty much have a twenty-five percent chance of it working, but the chemo will probably kill me."

"I will support you," I said, "no matter what you choose. It's okay to let go …"

"I can't do that," he said sweetly, with a smile. "I can't die knowing that I didn't fight."

The chemo appeared to work for a very short period of time, until that horrible week in February when the cold weather turned damp. Every moment of that week was with me forever, crystallized in my memory. I remember the phone call, my cell phone, around lunchtime, his stepfather calling to tell me that there had been a turn for the worst. When I got to the hospital, we cleared the room and I could see that Ayers was ready to say his good-byes; that he knew the fight was over.

"You are," he cried, "the best thing that has ever happened to me and don't ever forget it."

I lay in the hospital bed with him that afternoon, wanting to yell, "*stop!*" and bring it all to a halt. I did not know that his telling me I was the best thing that ever happened to him would be the last thing he said to anyone. For two days, he hung between life and death while we stayed with him, quietly telling him to let go, let go, let go, that we would be fine. When everyone had had a chance to say good-bye, Ayers finally let go, his now labored breathing coming to a quiet halt. His life ended so peacefully, so easily in fact, that even in my grief I could not believe death could be so peaceful. As I thought about it, I realized that death was much worse for the living. The last time I saw him, the corners of his mouth were turned up, the beginning of that mischievous smile that had taken me away such a short few years before.

My thoughts returned to Rick. He was everything I could want and he truly cared about me. He sent me flowers, chosen and arranged personally. He talked to me, held me, made me laugh, and made me want him. Could I deal with death again? Would I even have to deal with it again? Or could I just go with the beautiful feeling of loving someone again and let it lead me wherever? I could almost hear Ayers cheering for me. I could hear his voice again saying, "You go, boy". If anyone would encourage me to go on with my life and take this chance it would be him.

Then there was the always-nagging thought of deserving happiness after so much unhappiness. My religious upbringing would kick in at times like these, making me want to pray to god to justify my happiness, to somehow be sure that I was allowed to have it. Then I would immediately get scared, hoping that god didn't just hear me wishing happiness on myself, so that he or she could look down and say, "Silly little human, how dare you assume that you should be happy?" and take it all away again. I had always tried to figure out what I did to cause something so terrible to happen to me, just like my mother always tried to figure out what she did to make me gay. At times like these, solely focused on myself, I thought I was the only person in the world who had been faced with death and sadness. What would it feel like to be truly happy again? As I went to sleep, I imagined life in perfect arrangement with Rick.

CHAPTER 13

▼

UNMANNED

Learning that Rick had HIV took me by surprise, but dealing with it was something I had always done as a member of the gay community. It was one of those things that could be a possibility in the future, but strangely in the back of my head, far away from conscious thought. My conscious thoughts of HIV were usually for my own protection and detection. The test was a regular occurrence for me, but I never thought about the fact that someone would actually tell me they had it. In the middle of my thoughts about actually dealing with HIV in my own life, sitting at my desk at the office, Stuart called.

"Alexis," he said, "are you alone?"

"Bitch," I said in a low voice, under my breath, "you know I'm not alone at work."

"Well get up and close the door," Stuart commanded. "This just can't wait, Ho."

I got up immediately to close the door, glancing across the admin's bay to Madison's office where her chair was turned toward the window and her back was to me. Whenever I was on the phone and insisted on closing the door, she always managed to make some sort of smart comment.

"What's up your butt?" I demanded.

"Well," Stuart said slowly, indicating that he was ready to have a serious conversation. "I've never had an HIV test. Never. After all of the sex I've had, given and taken, you know, I've never been tested."

This admission hung in the air for a second, an admission that was foreign to me, the hypochondriac, so I wasn't sure how to respond. Of course I made a mental calculation about the last time I had been tested, probably six months before.

"Never?" I asked.

"Never," he replied.

"What brought this on?"

"Just thinking … I was thinking about this little dark haired Latin guy that I—"

"Okay," I interrupted, waiting for him to finish telling me some lurid detail about a random sexual encounter, but he stayed silent.

When Stuart became quiet, it was a sign that he wanted someone else to say something for a change.

"Maybe you should have a test," I said.

"When was your last one?" he asked.

"Six months ago. I do it regularly, you know."

"Will you come with me?"

"Um," I hesitated, and then realized that, for once, Stuart was calling on me for moral support instead of the other way around.

"Of course," I stated quickly. "And I'll have another test, too."

"I'm scared," Stuart said, "because I've done some things that were questionable, like the time when—"

"Okay, okay," I interrupted again. "Not over the company phone, huh?"

During the conversation I couldn't avoid thinking about Rick. Stuart's phone call and the ensuing drama were eerily identical and somehow were drifting into my life at the same time. I began to debate while Stuart was rattling on about one of his encounters, nicely bleeped out and sweetened up to avoid any reference to specific body parts or sexual acts. My debate was the thought of telling Stuart about Rick, to get an idea of how he would react, how he would advise me on the situation. Then I thought about Rick's privacy, how we had never spoken about who knew about him and who didn't and about the fact that we really weren't officially together yet. I decided not to say anything and went back to Stuart's story.

"…. um, blanked my, uh, you know," he was saying, "until I, well, um, did—"

"That's enough," I said. "Can we decide when and where this testing event is going to happen?"

"I have no clue," Stuart answered. "I could never ask my doctor for one. Isn't there a community clinic or something?"

"Yes," I replied, "but why would you have a doctor that you can't ask for an HIV test? That's sort of what they're for."

My doctor, a fortyish gay man with fabulous salt and pepper hair and warm hands, knew everything about me. Those warm hands had been just about everywhere, and I was always comfortable talking to him about the current condition of my body parts and my general health. In fact, during the last checkup, when I was buck-naked and Dr. Walker's hands were feeling around for a hernia, he reminded me that I was probably due for another test.

"I never felt comfortable with him," Stuart said, "so I don't talk to him about anything that personal. He's never seen me naked, for god's sake."

"Okay, well," I said, needing to get the conversation over with, "the clinic is near my place and takes walk ins until seven. Meet me at my place after work and I'll go with you."

I was almost sorry I agreed to go with him because we would have to go through some sort of explanation about why we were there and our sexual habits. I could not remember the last time Stuart really needed me, so this was obviously very important to him. I thought back over the times that he had done things with me and laughed. One Halloween, I was dying to do drag so Stuart took me to a beauty supply in his old neighborhood where the staff with their fabulous hair and nails greeted him warmly. He helped me select everything for my ensemble and even made the breasts for my outfit using panty hose and white rice to make them more realistic. Then there were the really heavy things, like coming to me as soon as Ayers died and just being there while I collected myself. This was friendship, and if Stuart needed me to help him protect himself, I was there.

He came to my place as agreed and we took my car about five blocks to the Community Health Center, a free clinic that ran on donations and charity events. The Center would deal with any health issue from anyone, so there was usually a nice mix of people hanging out there, among them the gay men like Stuart who couldn't talk to their doctors. Looking around I saw that even the HIV test was still a stigma, still something that people snuck around to get, an indication of why infection rates had gone down and then back up again. It seemed to me that people getting blood tests to confirm that they had cancer, diabetes, or high cholesterol didn't have to sneak around and weren't ashamed to mention it out loud. I felt bad for Stuart because he was obviously living with the fear of getting the test and admitting that he had gotten it. He quietly signed us in at the front desk and sat down next to me, not making eye contact with any of the other people in the room. As we sat in the waiting room, Stuart nervously fidgeted and played with his Blackberry repeatedly, and I tried to play nosy neighbor again and dig deeper.

"Did you ever ask any of the guys you had sex with what their HIV status was?" I asked, knowing that online hookups many times had a profile space for HIV status, although honesty was not on the top of the list when someone was looking for that kind of sex.

"No," he answered. "But I just figured they were so young and all, they didn't have time to have a history."

"Honey," I said smartly, "if a guy knows that he can do more than pee with his thing, he's old enough to have a history. I started thinking with my dick when I was about fourteen, didn't you?"

"Twelve," Stuart admitted. "I felt up Allison Dunn at the movies. Then I tried to feel up Tommy Blanco but he wouldn't let me."

I didn't reply to that one.

"One time," Stuart said, "I hooked up with this guy who was just out of college and working at one of the banks downtown. The condom came off and got stuck … well, up there."

"Come on," I said. "I'm not sure I want to hear this."

"Of course you do, nancy-boy," Stuart laughed. "I don't care how prudish you say you are, you always want to hear a good sex story."

"The condom got stuck, um, 'up there', on you or him?" I asked, laughing out loud at the fact that Stuart was, once again, right.

"Him," he continued. "And I kept going. I didn't, uh, finish there, if you know what I mean, but that little, um, incident has always made me afraid of karma. Do you believe in karma?"

"I don't know if I believe in karma," I answered, knowing that my answer was helping me work through yet another issue. "But I am afraid of it. Dumping Stephen made me afraid of karma because the whole relationship was wrong."

"Oh, get off your high horse, Queenie," Stuart said. "You're a human being. There's nothing wrong with sex."

A very large woman with a big Afro stepped out and yelled, "Mr. McGuire and Mr. Palini. Can you come back, please?"

As we walked back, I had to ask one final question: "And the condom?" I said in a whisper.

"The next day," Stuart whispered back as we followed Miss Afro, "he was sitting in a meeting and it sort of started to pop out. He had to excuse himself and extricate the thing."

Miss Afro noted my loud guffaw, smiled brightly and indicated a small, windowless room with a desk and a chair that was used for the bloodletting.

"Have a seat," she said. "My name is Lynnette. I'm going to take your blood today but I need to ask you some questions. First, are you two together?"

"God no," Stuart said, in a voice that ticked me off a tiny bit. "We're just girlfriends, Honey."

"So, Mr. McGuire," Lynnette said, "you are homosexual, correct?"

"That's quite an assumption," Stuart answered shortly, bucking for a conflict.

Lynnette's eyes peeked over her glasses and her eyebrows went up in a gesture that seemed to say, "cut the crap, I do this for a living."

"Yes." Stuart said quietly, "So is Mr. Palini."

"And how many sexual partners have you had, Mr. McGuire?" Lynnette inquired. "Ten? Twenty? More than twenty? I have to ask these questions for research purposes, you know."

"Well, more like twenty," Stuart replied, "but their age is usually around nineteen."

He winked at Lynnette who went right on with her questions. "And do you practice safe sex?" she asked Stuart. "Do you use a condom for oral and anal sex?"

"Anal sex, yes," he answered. "Oral sex, no."

"And what about you, Mr. Palini?" she turned her inquisition my way.

I had been mentally tallying the number of sexual partners I had encountered, including Stephen and Ayers, and was shocked to find that it was between ten and fifteen in the space of four short years. Lynnette helped me discover that I was a little ashamed about my sexual past.

"Well, about fifteen partners," I said and watched Stuart's eyebrows go up just like Lynnette's did earlier. "I use condoms for anal sex but not for oral sex."

"Fine," she answered. "Who's first?"

I was always amazed at the medical profession, that these people dealt with all kinds of disgusting things all day long and did not think a second thought about any of it. I was also certain that Lynnette had probably heard worse.

"I am," Stuart butted in and went over to the chair, turning a light shade of vomit green.

He winced as Lynnette pricked his arm with the needle and began drawing a few vials of blood. I watched what color was left in Stuart's face drain out and realized that this was as vulnerable as Stuart McGuire got. When Lynnette finished, he got up and stood near a small sofa at the back of the room. I had never had a problem with needles so Lynnette had an easy time with me. As she was drawing my blood, I watched Stuart teetering in the background, and, before I could react, Lynnette capped off the last vile and pulled the needle out of my arm rather quickly, leaving me with the cotton to hold over the injection site.

"Sorry Baby," she said to me. "He's goin' over."

As she said it, Stuart lurched backwards and somehow Lynnette in her bigness caught him like she was catching a fly ball in left field, and lowered him to the ground. I jumped up, afraid Stuart may have hurt himself.

"Don't worry, Baby," she said, kneeling over him, "he'll be fine."

I saw the color come back to Stuart's face as Lynnette helped him sit up.

"I hope you're driving," she said to me, and I nodded.

We got Stuart on the sofa for a few minutes and then Lynnette pronounced him able to leave. I knew he was embarrassed, so I said nothing.

"The doctor will call you in a few days," Lynnette informed us, "to let you know the results."

I knew that a phone call was good news, but a summons to go back to the office was probably bad news. I helped Stuart to the car and mentioned the phone call scenarios to him, trying to do anything but call attention to the fact that big Stuart McGuire just passed out in the arms of a black female nurse named Lynnette.

"I just passed out onto the bosom of a black female nurse," Stuart said as he sat next to me in the car, "and I liked it! Are you hungry? Let's go to Casa Eduardo for a margarita and some soft tacos, my treat."

I knew this was more of a commandment than a request, so I called Rick from the lobby at Casa Eduardo, just to say hello. He was again happy to hear from me and pointed out that I must still be in the running because I actually called him back. I did not tell Rick what we had been doing, because I still couldn't think of how to broach such a simple topic. I wondered how many guys had not called him back after he told them about the HIV and thought about how demoralizing that must have been. Not getting a call back after a couple of dates was bad enough, when there didn't seem to be an obvious reason except that the guy just didn't like you. I wondered how it felt to be rejected because of something like being HIV positive, and then thought about the fact that I was still thinking about rejecting Rick for the same reason.

CHAPTER 14

▼

MORE ABOUT SEX THAT I DIDN'T WANT TO KNOW

After three soft tacos and two margaritas, Stuart and I were in that place where we started talking whether we wanted to or not. His offer to treat me was a method of getting me to the talking place with the aid of adult beverages, so I tempered the drinking but resolved to talking Stuart out of his current difficulty.

"Okay," he said, putting his hands on the table. "Best sex ever story. Ayers doesn't count."

I had to think about that one. Sex with Stephen was always stimulating, but I think I was more taken with his body than with the way I actually felt about the sex, about that immediate electricity it was possible to have with someone who was strictly a sex partner.

"Well," I said slowly, "there was a Manlink hookup, and don't you dare tell *anyone* about this ..."

I went to Nashville for a continuing education course, spurred on by Madison in the first year after Ayers died. She had insisted that I go to get away and to take care of some regulatory training that we both had to have. At the last minute, Madison decided to go with me, so we drove up together and stayed in the same hotel, luckily not on the same floor. The second day of the three-day course let out around one in the afternoon, so Madison and I agreed to go back to the hotel, take a nap, and then meet for dinner around eight. I wasn't interested in napping so I logged on to Manlink as soon as I got back to my room. Within minutes, I had a couple of possible hookups and decided rather quickly that I wanted to have sex. Many times my entrance onto the website was the test of whether I was horny enough to degrade myself to the level of a dangerous Internet hookup and took hours to decide that I just didn't want to go that route. Since I was out of town, I reasoned, it was a perfect excuse to go trashy without even having to buy anybody drinks.

The best hit that afternoon was a guy who called himself Blubenz and put a few really hot photos on his profile, and not really much of anything by way of information, but our chat back and forth was quite cute. Of course I asked him to send photos via email, which he did, explaining that he had done some modeling both in the mainstream and in the gay media, which meant I could probably find him naked somewhere in print, and that he was also a real estate agent. The photos he sent were professionally done, showing him in sexy poses with jeans pulled down to his knees and a sleazy look on his face. I didn't respond right away because I was still thinking about the whole affair. When the next instant message popped up, it was Blubenz.

"I was in freakin' Sexy Zipper magazine!" he wrote, and then I realized that was where the photos came from. He called my hotel room and told me that his name was Daniel and that he really wanted to hook up with me. Of course I gave in, gave him directions, and called Madison immediately.

"What?" she said sleepily. "Why are you calling me?"

"If I don't meet you at eight sharp, get the cops, okay?" I instructed, excitedly.

"Fine," she replied and hung up.

When Daniel arrived at the hotel, I was pleasantly surprised by the good looking, polite, and well dressed guy at the door. He came in and we chatted for a few minutes until I interrupted to tell him how hot I thought he was and how I really wanted to get it on. I watched Daniel strip off his clothes, revealing the same well-kept body that was in the photos; six-pack abs, awesome ass, and arms that bulged with every motion. Daniel and I moaned and rolled our way through a few hours of fantastic sex, during which we discovered there was also an intellectual connection. When we were finished, we lay on the bed, at opposite ends of each other, my head just about at his crotch and my feet a few inches from his head, and talked about business, being gay, and oh, by the way, he had a partner who didn't mind if he had a little sex on the side, and maybe we could hook up for a three way. I knew this would probably not work for me, my limited experience with three-ways being total disasters, so I politely laughed it off with promises to keep in touch. As Daniel was getting dressed, I asked him about Sexy Zipper.

"Last August and September," he replied. "I had one photo in August and a spread in September. Check it out."

Right before getting ready for dinner, I ordered both issues of the magazine from the website. Madison grilled me about the whole thing, knowing what I had done and disapprovingly giving her blessing because we all had to get laid once in a while. I promised to show her the magazines when they arrived, which I did. The magazines stayed in my porno stash for a long time, to remind me of my afternoon hookup with a studly model.

"So no blue balls with blue Benz?" Stuart asked as the waitress brought our third round of margaritas.

"I wanted more details," he said.

"A good Southern boy doesn't go into detail," I said. "So what's your best sex story?"

Stuart launched into a much more graphic version of his best sex story, also an online hookup with a former marine in Arkansas, a beefy blonde, a true blonde, as Stuart so eagerly pointed out. He and Robert actually saw each other several times, and I was disappointed to find out that Stuart never told me about him, but Stuart insisted that the connection was purely physical. While Stuart was going on about the fact that Robert's house had a doorway at the end of a hallway with another doorway immediately perpendicular to it, so that Robert could prop his legs up in the hallway in between the two doorframes, I thought about the hookups I had allowed myself until I met Stephen. I always assured myself that I was just letting off steam and having sex to avoid being completely alone, which is what I ended up doing a few months before Stephen came along, anyway. Deep down inside, though, I was suffering from such a lack of confidence that getting guys interested was a twisted ego booster. I even ended up with a couple of dates from the Internet hookups, but the relationships never went anywhere. I concluded that the Manlink site was made up of guys that truly just wanted to have sex, and those of us who hid our loneliness acting like guys who truly just wanted to have sex. There were some very hot encounters during that time in my life, sexual experiences that far exceeded my expectation and helped me decide what the next real relationship would absolutely have to be like, which of course, did not happen when Stephen showed up. I was unsure about Rick but I liked the whole package. Maybe at this point in my life was where those past indiscretions would actually start to make sense. Stuart was still going on, so I picked up the last few words and acted suitably impressed.

"… yep, four parts water and one part Chlorox disinfects everything," he was saying, "and I *do* mean *everything* … this way we could do the tongue and lips thing whenever we wanted to, we just kept the spray bottle close at hand."

I couldn't imagine what disgusting things I had missed but was thankful that my mind was able to wander without my face betraying a moment of distraction.

"You know," Stuart said, "you've never told me if you are a bottom or a top."

"Do I have to?" I asked.

"Yes," he replied.

"Versatile," I said, smiling coyly, using the term that applied to any of us who would give or take based on the current sexual situation. I knew that this was the way it had been with Ayers and with Stephen, so I was speaking the truth.

"What were you with Disposable Boy?" Stuart inquired nosily.

"Top mostly," I explained, "except when he would make a big deal about feeling emasculated. Of course, he didn't use that word but that's what he meant. He was actually pretty good at it. What about you?"

"Top all the time," Stuart said, completely negating his fear over the HIV test.

"Liar, liar," I replied. "Girdle's on fire."

"Okay," he said. "Then *vers-a-tile*. There. Are you happy?"

I just smiled and took another swig of my margarita, remembering that Casa Eduardo's margaritas were made in a machine and were so watered down that I could drink six of them before they made me drunk.

"So," Stuart said in his kiss-and-tell voice, "what was the whole piercing thing like with Disposable Boy?"

"Strangely hot," I answered, recalling how it really turned me on the first time I saw it in action.

The second sexual encounter with Stephen, a few days after our first night of drunken sex, was a slower, more deliberate act, although Stephen was still fast about it. I left the lights on so Stephen could show me the piercing, which he had no problem doing. He let me feel it, twist it around, play with it in general while he groaned with pleasure, explaining in between gasps that it was like no stimulation a guy could get. The piercing grew on me, turning me on every time I saw Stephen naked, making me pat myself on the back for becoming so broad-minded. The problem with the piercing, I explained, was that Stephen had to pee sitting down like a girl, and that if he took it out the chances were that the hole would never close up.

"Sounds worth it," Stuart said. "Especially to get an excuse to daintily sit upon the throne whenever you have to take a leak. Did it, um, squirt, every which way, too?"

"Um, no," I answered sarcastically.

By the time we got the check we were both laughing hard from making penis piercing jokes, everything from getting patted down at the airport to not going around the MRI at the local hospital, because you wouldn't want to get your thing trapped in a magnet. Then the conversation turned serious again.

"We've just entered no-man's land," said Stuart.

"What do you mean?" I asked.

"Well," he explained, "we're in between the test and knowing for sure. It feels like no man's land. How do you deal with this?"

"I'm not sure," I replied, honestly. "You know how I worry about every god-damned thing. I'm not sure how I get through it without a stroke or a heart attack."

"Did you ever think," he said, "even during the best sex ever, that this could be the time your life changes forever? Did you really and truly think about the possibilities of HIV at the time? When that hot guy was er, finishing, did you think about it?"

It was amusing that I really had not thought about it until after the fact, after the guy had gone home and I was alone again, but now, here I was actively partic-ipating in this conversation knowing that Rick and his HIV were there right in the back of my head. Here I was thinking about the fact that HIV alone could keep me from falling in love. Now that the events of today had caused me to look at my sexual life from fifty thousand feet instead of seven or eight inches I was left wondering if one of those had been the one, even though I was careful. After all, HIV could take a while to show up in a test.

"Did you ever look back," Stuart was saying, "and think that this guy, the one you were with at the time, could be the one who may have infected you?"

"I have," I said, "but I think there are people who know where it came from, especially if they may have acted irresponsibly one time. Then again, there are probably people who have no idea where it came from because they practice risky behavior all the time."

"I'm scared, Alex," Stuart said quietly. "I know I shouldn't be. I also know it's the Twenty-first Century and we can deal with this if it's bad news. It's just a lit-tle freaky, that's all."

"I know," I said, and again briefly considered telling him about Rick, and then again decided against it.

As we drove back in, I saw Rick's light on and wondered what he was doing, wondered if he was alone or if he was with someone, because he may have been dating and not telling me about it. I got jealous for a second and knew then that

I was not going to say no because of Rick's self-labeled baggage, but I was going to have to wade through that scary region of my brain where all of the doubt resided before I could make up my mind clearly. I hoped that he would hang on long enough.

CHAPTER 15

▼

MEETIN' THE MAN

On the day of Stephen's party, I woke up, went for a run, and ended up on the sofa watching *America's Test Kitchen* on PBS. The mindless testing of the right mustard and the correct width of string to tie a pork loin kept my mind off of what had been going on that week. Rick was so patient and continued to see me, coming over for dinner, having cocktails, or having coffee in the morning like Lucy and Ethel. The fact that he was HIV positive did not have any adverse effect on my attraction to him, so after a few cocktails I was always ready to jump him. The thought of falling for him and then losing him was the one that stuck around, although that day it was dressed with mustard and tied with a string. Just thinking about losing someone else made the pain come back, that lump in my throat that just wouldn't go away, making me feel like I was going to either choke or cry.

So if Rick and I could make a go of it, what would he think of me? I could imagine loving the man and then watch him realize that life with Alex was not a country fair cakewalk. I was a perfectionist about everything. My shoes could not touch in the closet, the pillows on the sofa had to be just so, cleaning was done every Saturday, and dirty dishes did not sit around more than an hour. What if Rick couldn't stand it? Was I scared of what I perceived as making a sacrifice and then being rejected myself? Ayers always left a dirty trail, whether it was his clothes, his bag, his food, whatever. I could always tell when he was home because of the trail, and I always went behind him with the dust rag. I'm sure it drove him nuts, but he put up with it because he loved me. Rick didn't seem to worry about things like that, even though as a person he seemed to be very neat. As the people on TV made the decision about some off-brand French mustard, the phone rang.

"I get really gassy sometimes," said Rick, using his little boy voice.

"Farty gassy or belchy gassy?" I asked back.

"Both," he replied. "That's the next deal-breaker."

"I don't think so," I said. "But I am a scary neat freak. If we got married, I'd have to follow you around with a can of Lysol."

"I'll bet you fart, too," he said, again in the little boy voice, "but I wouldn't mind."

It struck me that with this simple comment Rick was just trying to make me see the normalcy between us in spite of the obvious pink elephant in the room.

"When do you want me for cocktails?" he asked, knowing that Madison and Stuart would be chomping at the bit to meet him.

"Around eight," I answered, and resisted the urge to ask him over for yet another cup of coffee. Stuart always said that his grandmother, a former flapper, told him to *cherchez l'homme*, to grab the man while you still could, before he moved on to another. How many cups of coffee would Rick go through before he gave up?

"Okay," Rick said. "I've got to go to the office and get some work done, so I'll see you then."

After we hung up, I did an Internet search on HIV statistics. It was obvious that medical advancements continued to improve lives and life expectancy, because one article I read stated bluntly that an American with HIV could expect to live on average twenty-five years from diagnosis. The math for Rick entered my head and then I stopped myself. I had always been one to see the glass half empty, literally. After all, if you take a few gulps from a full glass you are effectively emptying it, right? I felt that I was viewing Rick as a glass with a few sips out of it. My obsessive-compulsive nature could always be counted on to put a nail in the cogs as it just did. Rick didn't ask for this. He admitted that it was one stupid mistake that cost him. I wondered what it would be like to know that something lurking in your body was possibly the thing that would kill you. After numerous articles and plenty of symptom lists, I felt more confused than ever. Every thought in my head was a "what if" again, my thoughts always heading in the direction of the things I feared but that wouldn't necessarily come to be. Whenever there was something that I really wanted, like when I decided to go out for a fraternity in college, I dreaded actually doing it. I was so good at almost convincing myself to skip the chance, but when I got into whatever it was, like pledging, I ended up enjoying it. I kept thinking about all of the decisions I made based on the fear of the "what if". As in most times of severe stress, I went to sleep and didn't wake up until my alarm went off at seven o'clock that evening.

I barely had enough time to shower and pick out something to wear, which was always a trial, especially since I was alone. Gay couples, I always asserted, were great for fashion, not only because you could share your clothes but because you were more than likely to get a fair assessment of your look for no charge. Ayers and I fought many times over his Vera Charles-like candid clothing opinions, but I always managed to make a splash when he was around. I changed clothes about three times, thinking that one outfit made me look fat while another one suspiciously negated my ass. I finally picked my Earl Jean low-rise jeans and a Gucci plunging neckline t-shirt.

"Just enough cleavage to be sexy," I said as Stuart's familiar knock sounded on the back door. Stuart knocked on doors just like my grandmother and then walked straight in calling out, "woo hoo!" just like any seventy-something Southern belle. He stood in the kitchen doorway, all six feet three inches of him. Stuart always battled weight but capitalized on the fact that many young guys liked a big bear. He did his best Hollywood starlet-in-the-doorway pose.

"Uh huh, Doreen," he mocked in his Feathers voice. "You invite me over here to meet this new hot man and you ain't gonna serve me no liquor?"

"Girl," I shot back, "hold that whalebone corset. I had to scrub everything down really good and it took a while."

"Well, it should have, the way you've been carrying on lately. You didn't go and get the clap or something, did you?" Stuart asked in his humorous yet serious tone.

"If I remember correctly," I said as I went to the bar to begin mixing yet another round of drinks. "You were the one that got crabs from Donna Merriweather's husband, were you not?"

Stuart, in one of his sluttier moments, had a one-night-stand with a married man, which was not so unusual in the South, but it was unusual that the man turned out to be the husband of someone he worked with.

"We agreed we weren't going to bring that up again," Stuart snapped, and then added with his arms upturned like a Baptist at a revival, "but the crabs were worth it. Goddamn!"

As I handed Stuart his martini, Absolut straight up with two olives, Madison knocked daintily on the back door.

"Don't talk about the whole HIV test thing," Stuart instructed, obviously over the waiting and ready to have a good time.

"Right," I said, not wanting to bring it up again and surprised at how well I had ignored the subject over the past few days, even with Rick.

When I went to the door, I was as usual not surprised at how fantastic Madison looked. She was wearing a brown silk sundress with spaghetti straps and a plunge that seemed to eject her breasts right out of it. She immediately kissed me on the cheek and started our usual fag to hag sucking up. When Madison learned that she was a fag hag, she was almost disappointed, because, she explained, fag hags were those big girls with bad fashion sense and ugly, overdone, fake fingernails. Stuart and I explained to her that being a fag hag was a compliment. Gay guys like us, with fabulous lives, clothes, and snappy comebacks, were very choosy about the women we incorporated into our lives. We picked women who were just like us, only the gay man was trapped in a woman's body. She began wearing her label like a badge, and had even always considered designing her own clothing line to be called "Hag". Of course, we had yet to see the first sketch.

"If I were a gay man," she said.

"If I were a straight man," I replied as Madison licked her lips and rolled her eyeballs up into her head.

"Honey," Madison drawled, "this better be worth it. I've almost wet myself twice tonight thinking about seeing Marilyn Clark's house and about meeting this new hottie you've got the cranks for."

Madison could always be counted on to be frank about her biological conditions. At work she could discreetly lean over in a meeting and whisper, "Aunt Flow is here." When I first met her, she explained that after her first child she went back to work while still lactating. Of course a client brought a baby into the office and Madison was very descriptive about how her boobs had leaked on her desk. This was not a person to hide anything from.

"And," Madison continued, "I know that something is just a little off. I can't put my finger on it, but of course you boys are better at fingering things than I am."

She made a dramatic show of hugging and kissing Stuart as I mixed her cocktail, thinking that my mother would have a fit if she knew how much I was drinking lately. My nerves were twisted. All I could think about was Rick meeting these two. Both Madison and Stuart were uncanny judges of character and people, whereas my skill sometimes lacked. One night at a bar, I was tipsy and began a conversation with a really good-looking guy. The conversation went on for about two and half minutes, until Stuart walked up, looked at me, pointed his finger, and said very plainly, "No". I never knew if the guy was a creep or not, but I always trusted Stuart. Now I was afraid that he or Madison would figure out this big secret before I was ready to tell them.

"I think we're all acting like moronic children," I interjected, "because we're clamoring to go to a party given by a drugged-out grunge boy at his dead mother's house. Are we this desperate for some kind of twisted, depraved action?"

Madison and Stuart were frozen over the edges of their glasses with pursed lips, lips that were trying to sip and laugh at the same time. Madison spoke first.

"Honey," she said patronizingly, "you started it. Besides, I have two kids and a husband at home. How the hell else am I supposed to get some drama in my life? Benjamin threw up a hot dog the other day because his older brother made him laugh too hard. That's the only drama I get. Be this evening depraved, twisted, or immature, I plan to enjoy it!"

Stuart piped in. "Get your knickers out of their twist."

He then opened my hall closet, pulled out a beat-up old feather boa that had been in there since 1996, wrapped it around his head and shouted, "Life is a banquet, darling!"

I gulped half of my martini and relaxed, knowing that I was just as interested in being immature as they were. We were laughing together when I heard Rick knock and open the door. When he walked in, we all stared dumbly. He was wearing a green shirt, with long sleeves, and jeans, along with some really butch brown Gucci boots. The green shirt, with one extra button undone, made his green eyes stand out so that they were the first thing we saw, followed by his chest. The combination of this startling effect and his bright smile made him absolutely gorgeous. All of us were captivated. Madison was frozen mid-sip, Stuart's mouth, usually busy, was open but not saying anything, and the old boa was hanging halfway over his face. I was proudly eyeing what could be the prized catch, but then the reality came back into my head and I moved into action.

"Hi there," I said, moving forward to give Rick a hug. "Excuse these two," and, as I said it, smacked Stuart on the arm. "They look like my evil stepsisters."

I introduced them and Rick reacted warmly, kissing both of them on the cheek. I handed Rick his cocktail and decided to let the meeting unfold.

"So, Rick," asked Madison in her business style, "what do you do for a living?"

"I run Gilroy's Florists, on Union. My parents own it but they sent me here to run it," he explained.

"Actually," I spoke up, "it's more than that. He's the C.O.O. of this floral empire that his mother started. Are you jealous yet?"

"Well, you are just fine, mister!" yelled Stuart before Rick could respond, finally unwrapping the boa from his head.

This was going well. As they chatted, I thought about the first time I introduced Ayers to Stuart. Stuart put his arm around Ayers and walked away with him, giving me the wink on his way. The two of them went to the bar, had a drink together while I danced, and then came back as thick as thieves. The first and only time I ever saw Stuart cry was when Ayers died. Stuart always knew what to say at every moment, for every occasion, but for this one he was speechless. When he saw Ayers in the casket, Stuart truly lost it and I had to walk him outside. I always wondered if Stuart had a thing for Ayers, but I never let on. There was one certainty that always stayed with me, even after Ayers was gone: he was always mine and I never had a reason to doubt it.

Stuart drove us all to the party in his big Cadillac, aptly named the S.S. McGuire, this huge silver thing with delicious leather seats and plenty of gadgets to play with. When we pulled up outside Stephen's house, we saw cars parked everywhere, even a few on the lawn.

"Marilyn Clark is rolling over in her grave," said Madison in a half-whisper, as if someone could hear us. "It went from yard of the month to parking lot within a few weeks."

Stuart jockeyed the S.S. McGuire into a spot on the street, right behind an old panel van that could have been a Holiday Inn on wheels. As we got out, the van's back door opened and a cute young guy, zipping his pants, jumped out. We could see another guy inside, not quite as cute and not as dressed. The four of us shot hilarious looks at each other, wondering if this is what we would find inside.

"Maybe all of this trash is happening outside and not inside," I said and continued nervously in Alex run-on. "But then again this whole thing could be animal house and why don't we just skip it and go have dinner at the Club Room in the Peabody?"

"Shuh-uh," replied Rick in the gayest voice I had heard from him yet. "This has got to be good. Where's your sense of adventure?"

"My sense of adventure is on a Go Gay Tour Bus in Italy, not at a queer frat party," I shot back.

Rick reached over and tweaked my ear as we walked up to the front door. Madison flung the door open like she was walking into her own house, and there, right in the front hall with a glass of champagne and the Tattinger bottle to match, was Stephen. Right behind him, with a hand clasped a little too tightly on his shoulder, was Nick. I immediately went back to the conversation that Rick and I had at the restaurant, when he told me about Nick and described him as

Stephen's latest screw. From the way Nick was gripping him I could tell it was true. I also immediately wondered what it was like to be "Nick and Rick" on the answering machine.

"Hi, dudes," Stephen said as he reached over to hug me, Nick's grasp barely coming away from his shoulder. "I'm glad you could come. And I see you've brought your posse."

Nick was doing a sort of hover in the background, so I decided to be polite like my great-great Aunt Melanie taught me.

"Nick, Stephen," I said. "This is my great friend Stuart and my even greater friend Madison. She's greater because her boobs are really out there, aren't they? And you both know Rick."

Nick acknowledged Stuart and Madison with a smile and gave a glum look to Rick. There was an awkward silence that lasted for about three seconds, until a seven foot drag queen propelled herself into the hallway to ask Madison when she got her breasts done. Rick and Stuart went to find the bar and Madison was now getting killer makeup tips from the drag queen, named Georgia Powers. Keeping my eye on Rick, I walked down the entrance hall and into one of the hallways that opened onto the bedrooms. There were people everywhere, drinking, talking, and laughing, so the party seemed like it was pretty normal. I already needed to find the toilet, since the vodka from my first martini was about to make its first appearance.

All of the doors were closed, and I could not remember where the bathroom was. Contrary to Southern etiquette I just started opening doors. The first door I opened was a linen closet that smelled nicely of lavender. When I opened the second door, I couldn't even gasp. There, on the bed, ass-up and spread-eagle, was a naked guy with a tribal tattoo on his back, right on his tan line. Standing over the dresser, inhaling through a rolled up bill, was another naked guy who I strangely recognized as the friend of Stephen's that approached Rick and me at Station 69. He had piercings in his nipples, his belly button, and had added a new one on his eyebrow. He looked up, saw me, and smiled. Piercing Boy was still kind of cute, and he gave me a nod as I noticed that his hair was much less greasy than the last time I saw him.

"Dude," he said, "you wanna join us? George over here is hot. We can take turns."

"No thanks," I said, laughing nervously. "I think I'm in enough trouble as it is."

"Whatever dude," piercing boy replied. "But I always thought you were hot and now that Stevie is all about Nick you're a free man."

"Okay. Well," I was barely able to get the words out, "maybe when you hit eighteen I'll think about it."

Before he could react I slammed the door and considered finding a tree out in the back yard. The way things were going I thought that I would probably run across Bigfoot or something equally as bizarre if I went out there. I made my way to the large living room, where more normal people were drinking cocktails, flirting, and talking. I saw Rick, Nick, and Stephen in one corner, and noted that Stuart and Madison had now been introduced to a trio of drag queens. One of them was squeezing Madison's left boob, remarking about how you could never tell that two babies had breast fed off of it. Stephen walked away, giving me those sad eyes as he went, heading toward the sex hallway. As I sidled close to Rick and Nick, I overheard their whispers.

"You mean you didn't tell him?" asked Rick with his teeth gritted.

"No, why should I?" Nick fired back. "It doesn't mean shit to any of us now. So you've both had me and Dolly over there, so what?"

He made eyes in my direction when he mentioned Dolly, although I couldn't figure out why he decided to call me that. I guess blonde hair and a decent rack made everybody a Dolly in Nick's mind. I broke in between them and cattily remarked, "Dolly's back."

Nick looked sheepish and then apologized, explaining that he was just being dramatic.

"He didn't tell Stephen about how we're all connected," Rick explained, his voice having taken a more cordial tone. "So I was just trying to find out why."

"You know damned well why," hissed Nick. "So I don't even want to talk about it."

Nick stalked off and I gave Rick a puzzled look.

"Nick is violent," Rick said flatly. "That's basically it. He beat me up a couple of times and he's afraid that if Stephen knows we were together he'll try to get the dirt. I'm not gonna tell him, it's just something that I guarantee he's gonna find out on his own."

"How did you end up …" I started a question but was interrupted by Rick.

"That's another conversation," he said sternly.

Rick grabbed my hand and led me back into the sex hallway where he opened doors and backed out with a laugh a couple of times until he found the lavender linen closet. He pulled me inside, wrapped his arms around my waist, and we made out like teenagers hiding from their parents. It was moments like this that made me consider just giving up my obsessive worry about a relationship with Rick and give in. I was on the edge of falling for him, and his grabbing me like this made my head spin not to mention making me balls-out horny for him and only him. In my younger days, horny was my body's way of telling me to have sex, regardless of whether I was with someone or not. Lately, though, horny was attached to a specific person and not a feeling or the fantasy of having sex with someone I had just met online or in a bar. It was funny that thoughts of being with other guys did not enter my head anymore, as if I was telling myself that it would have to be Rick or no one. As he kissed me, the doubt still hung in my mind like the smoke in the hallway. I was also obsessing over the fact that there seemed to be more to the relationship with Nick than met the eye. Then, for one split second, I let myself go and gave in to Rick's hot kiss and hotter embrace, and it felt good, until Georgia Powers opened the closet door looking for tissue. I was relieved because I wasn't sure how long that hot embrace could last before it became something else. I didn't give it up right away for Ayers and I wasn't going to give it up right away for Rick. It seemed, though, at that moment, deep down inside, my decision had been made.

CHAPTER 16

▼

BECOMING HUMAN

The S.S. McGuire was rowdy on the way back to my place, because Madison and Stuart were witnesses to the drag queens and the closet. Madison was tipsy enough to later leave her car in my parking lot and let Stuart drive her home, so her lips were loose.

"I like you, Rick," she said, pointing her finger at his general direction in the back seat, "even though you let floosey goosey here con you into making out in a closet like a couple of Baptists at summer camp."

I sat up, began to puff up like a chicken, ready to do battle, when Rick laughed and went along with it.

"Well," he said, "I've been trying to get him to make out in the closets at my apartment but he won't."

"That's all right," slurred Madison. "Honey, you hold out as long as you want to. Rick's a nice guy and he's smart, too. He'll wait for you. Damn, I shouldn't have had that last martini. I think that girl at the bar had the hots for me."

"That would be easy," remarked Stuart, "seeing as your tits are out there like a 'for rent' sign."

"Anyway," Madison continued, as if she were still in the middle of a complete thought, "Rick, just don't hurt him. We're in the business of protecting our friend because he's gone through too damned much anyway. You hurt him, I'll cut your balls off."

After she said this, Madison gave Rick one of her best Martha Stewart smiles and started singing along, badly, with Deborah Cox, and Stuart joined her while Rick critiqued both of their vocal styles in reality TV style. Somehow I managed to tune out the rest of the banter in the S.S. McGuire, thinking about the first time Ayers and I got drunk together. Stuart drove us that particular night from the clubs, where we drank beer, chased it with whiskey, and smoked pot. We were all pretty giddy by the time Stuart dumped us out at our apartment, so Ayers and I quickly went upstairs to have sex before we passed out, which we did right in the middle of the foreplay. When we woke up a couple of hours later, naked and stuck together, we laughed so hard that we couldn't speak. It could have been one of those things that couples look back on with embarrassment, but Ayers turned it into a joke that lasted for the rest of our relationship, taking it to the point of pretending to pass out during sex just for a laugh. He had a way of turning weird situations into something laughable and enjoyable. Ayers helped me realize that laughing at myself was healthy, although after he died I had a great deal of trouble trying to laugh at anyone's expense, much less my own.

Rick and I were drunk enough to want to keep blabbing, so we went up to my place and I fixed coffee. While I was pouring, Rick snuck off and came back with the Bailey's, just what we needed to top off a night of drinking.

"We're too old for this," I said. "You know it's gonna hurt in the morning."

"No pain, no gain," laughed Rick.

"So," I said, "does any of this scare you?"

"Falling for you doesn't scare me," he said, "but the thought of leaving you does. But then again, I'd be dead."

"Oh ha ha," I replied. "I'm sure you might try to haunt me."

"Yeah," he snapped back. "I'd hang out in your bathroom so you wouldn't be able to poop."

Rick and I had, even before the farty-gassy conversation, even before sexual intimacy, securely reached the potty stage so he knew about my need for absolute privacy in the toilet. I told him that bathrooms should be seen and not heard. I also told him that when I was searching for an apartment, I turned one down because it had a bathroom that opened out on the living room. I always believed that this neurotic bathroom behavior stemmed from a photograph my father took of me sitting on the toilet when I was about three. I was wearing a little coat with a hood, but I left the hood up and pulled my little pants down. This great position survived over the years to become a source of hilarity at every family gathering.

"Really," he said seriously, "my fear is of becoming a burden. I don't want someone to have to take care of me. You know how proud I am of being self-sufficient. I'm not sure I could lose my independence."

"Understandable," I said, both of us knowing that I spoke from experience.

"I have good days and bad days," he went on. "Sometimes I'm totally freaked out and scared about what the next day might bring. It's like being struck with fear that has no tangible source, like waking up in the middle of the night afraid but not quite sure what you're afraid of. Then I go all normal again. My shrink in Atlanta put me on Paxil but I hated it. It made me feel like I wasn't living my own life. My ears rang for a week when I went off of it. Now I try to control my own emotions."

"You show emotion well," I remarked, "but you know I don't. It's my mother's rule of not letting them see you cry. I come from an Italian family, but they're emotional about their ravioli and not their feelings. Strange."

Looking at the clock on the microwave, I saw that it was nearly two in the morning. Suddenly, there was a knock on the back door. Rick looked up and indicated that we would both go to answer it. When we peeked through the curtain, we saw Stephen, his head strangely down, his chin sitting on his chest. He looked up, and to our horror had a black eye, a gash on his forehead, and blood running from his nose. I immediately thought that he had been in an accident or had gotten into a brawl with one of the Goldilocks Gang as he stood there, staring at us until I opened the door to let him in.

"Jesus, dudes," he complained. "I thought you weren't going to let me in."

"Well, Dude," I said sarcastically, "it is almost two in the AM. What the hell happened to you?"

Stephen paused for a moment, much too long to make us believe that his explanation would be the truth. Stephen's lies, just like the crying on command, were hilarious to watch, because they were obviously unplanned but even after a major whopper of a fib, he could smile and make anyone forget what he just said. He stammered, and then got that pouty look that came before the tears.

"Nick," Rick said out of the blue. "Did Nick do this to you?"

Stephen's next sobby outburst told us that this was the case. I wondered for a moment how Nick managed to get violent with someone as strapping as Rick. Then I thought about how endlessly annoying Stephen could be, but never once had I felt like hitting him.

"I told him that he needs to lay off," he stammered, "l-lay off of you two."

"That's it?" I asked. "This caused him to rough you up like this?"

"N-no," Stephen said, shuddering, while Rick hung in the background. "When he t-told me that he and Rick were together, I called h-his ass out on it. I told him that h-h-he either needed to be with me or lay off you t-two."

Stephen stopped, so Rick pulled himself off of the kitchen wall impatiently.

"And?" Rick snapped.

"And he p-pushed me," Stephen started to get emotional again and then got himself together to finish his story. "He pushed me out of the back patio door. I hit the goddamned ground so hard that I couldn't fucking breathe. I got up and swung at him. I m-missed."

"Obviously," I remarked in my out loud voice.

Rick handed Stephen a bag of frozen peas, and Stephen stared at it with a dazed look.

"I was making succotash," Rick snapped sarcastically, "so I wanted you to hold those for me. For chrissakes, put that on your eye and it'll keep it from swelling so much."

I wasn't sure what to do. I still needed time to think through it all but I looked at Stephen and felt a strange sense of sympathy. I could believe his whining would make even the Pope think about taking a swing, but I could not imagine that someone as new in his life as Nick would actually beat him up that brutally. I did not want to send Stephen home because I was afraid that Nick would take another swing at him. I also didn't want him at my place because I was a tiny bit afraid that Nick would show up. I looked at Rick, apparently in a way that betrayed my bewilderment.

"Let him sleep on the sofa," he advised, "because Nick won't come here. Once he's had his shot, he doesn't try again. Not for a day or so anyway. I'm going home. Call me if you need anything."

I didn't want to see him go, but I guessed that he needed to be away from the drama. At the door, I put a grim smile on my face.

"Is this an example of the good taking care of the stupid?" I whispered.

"You could say that," Rick answered, "although I'm not really sure who's who right now."

He squeezed my shoulder, winked, and went down the stairs. I was finally at the point where I could resist Stephen, especially since he was a bloody mess. I helped him clean up, dabbing some peroxide on the cut over his eye and wiping his face. I could tell, for once, that Stephen was grateful for the attention.

"Don't bother getting any pillows or anything," he instructed. "I've already been enough trouble and I ran your boyfriend off. I just don't understand why these things keep happening to me."

"Let's not talk about that," I replied, "so you can get some sleep. You know what?"

"What?" Stephen said, suspiciously.

"I'm sorry if I led you on about us," I said slowly. "If I made you believe that it could have been more than it was. And I'm sorry for using you."

"Using me?" Stephen inquired. "I thought I used you."

"Whatever," I said. "You deserve to be wanted for you and not just for the body and the attitude, and I'm sorry if I made you feel that way."

"Thanks," Stephen answered, sincerely, and closed his eyes. I could tell he meant it. In a few minutes, he was asleep, probably the first time he fell asleep with both eyes closed in a few days. I stood there for a few minutes watching him. I thought about Rick and how quickly he took off, and wondered why. Then I thought about the progress I had just made in a very few minutes. I wasn't feeling guilty for Stephen anymore, now that I had been able to show him some genuine kindness. I actually wanted to show him that someone cared about him more than superficially, how gay guys could actually be friends. As usual, the fact that I was making friends with someone I had once had sex with made it a little easier. So many of us had ulterior motives or felt strange when we were friends with a man that we had not known carnally. My gay shrink, in a weird inverse of therapy, once told me about the time he sat in a room with his partner over and over again with the same three friends for years until one day he looked around and realized that they had each had sex with his partner at some time or another before he came into the picture. With this arrangement, Stephen and I could be sure that there would be no awkward attractions or underlying tension brought on by feelings, physical or otherwise. I moved from horny predator to real person where Stephen was concerned, and saw that I really wanted him to succeed somehow.

"Now if I could just figure out the rest of this shit," I said out loud.

I put my favorite fuzzy blanket over Stephen and went to bed.

CHAPTER 17

▼

REALIZATION

"Alex?" Stephen whispered, peeking in the doorway of my bedroom.

I lifted my face from the pillow, which was wet with my drunken slobber, thinking that I had just put the blanket over him. The light was coming through the windows, and the clock said it was ten something. In my haze, I could barely make it out. I smelled coffee and wondered what was going on.

"I walked over to Starbucks and got you a latte," Stephen informed me. "Just like you like it."

I sat up, wanting to play hide the body again but then not bothering. I assumed that the new terrain of our relationship could allow me to show a little skin without feeling awkward. He sat down on the side of the bed and handed me the coffee, which was just the right temperature to drink. As I shook off sleep and sipped, Stephen started talking hesitantly.

"I, um, need you to listen to me," he said, seriously. "I've been thinking that I need to do something about my problems. I can't seem to stop doing coke and drinking too much. I'm scared, because last night I didn't know what I was doing. Maybe if I hadn't been doing it, I wouldn't have made Nick so mad. Dude, I need to get some help."

Before the fight with Nick the previous night, Stephen explained, he looked around at his party, and in a moment of clarity, saw that the place was like a drug outlet store, where you could get whatever you wanted for next to nothing or, in his case, for free. He looked around and saw the crowd, and as the clarity wore off, wanted to have as much fun as they were having. After a few lines, Stephen was feeling way up yet agitated, thinking that maybe he would try to get Nick to have sex in one of the closets or out by the pool like some of the other guests, in an attempt to release some energy. The agitation, as I had noticed with Stephen, came out like a mosquito buzzing around your nose, so someone with Nick's borderline personality did not stand much of a chance of staying calm. After one pass, Nick walked away, disappearing while Stephen said goodbye to his last remaining guests. When he found Nick again, he unwittingly crossed the line and the pushing started. As much as I wanted to say, "I told you so," I just nodded in agreement. For Stephen to come to this realization was a step that needed to go on uninterrupted.

"I did some research this morning," he continued, "and I want you to help me check into the county addiction recovery center. They have counseling for gay people and I really think it could help. I'm at the end of my rope, Alex."

I still couldn't fathom what he was telling me, but I knew that the person talking to me was the real Stephen, the semi-mature, educated guy I thought he was.

"Last night," he said, "you showed me you really care. Rick, too. You guys are successful guys and you do it without any help. You can take me there today and I'll stay for a few days or whatever."

The phone rang.

"Hey, you," said Rick, "what's going on over there? Are you two okay?"

I looked at Stephen, who nodded, knowing that it was Rick on the line.

"We're fine," I said. "Stephen has decided to get some help."

Rick came over immediately and sat with Stephen while I called the recovery center. I suppose we were both afraid he would run, so we silently agreed to make sure that didn't happen. This was not where I had hoped to be on Sunday morning, but I hoped that we were truly helping Stephen.

We went by his house to help him pick up a few things and were amazed at the sight. The Holiday Inn on wheels was still there, and there were no signs of anything crazy in the front yard. But when we stepped inside, the place was trashed, cans, bottles, plastic bags all over, flowers trampled on the floors, glasses and dishes piled up in the kitchen. In the master bedroom, where Stephen's things were, there were even a few used condoms lying around, at which Rick remarked that it was a good thing the crowd was still using protection. Judging from these leftovers, I could see where Stephen's feeling of being out of control could have come from. The only thing missing, I reasoned, was naked people splattered on the furniture.

The recovery center apparently had a light load, which was a surprise, judging from the number of people at Stephen's house the night before that may have made a change of heart just as he did. Stephen handled himself very professionally and paid for a single room without hesitation. While we were getting Stephen set up in his room at the rehab center, he opened up again.

"Maybe if I can get over this," he said, "I can make things work with Nick. I really like him."

Rick looked puzzled.

"Sorry, man," Stephen said. "I'm sorry if that makes you uncomfortable."

"Not uncomfortable for me," Rick replied, "uncomfortable for you. What you saw last night is him, not you. It doesn't take much to get him mad and then it's all over. The first time that happened to me, I remember thinking that it couldn't possibly be real."

They had been arguing about something small, but the argument then escalated to shouting, and then screaming. Rick turned to walk out on him, down a long hallway in their house. The floors were terrazzo, he explained, so they were slick, cold, and hard. Nick came after him, grabbing him by the shoulder and spinning him around, and then shoving him as hard as he could. When Rick hit the terrazzo he fell flat on his back and was more than momentarily stunned. When he saw Nick coming to stand over him, he began to slip and slide backwards, trying to get away.

We were frozen, staring at Rick telling the story, his face painfully blank.

Nick kicked him in the ribs while screaming loudly about his lack of respect and understanding. Rick could not get a word out, he remembered, and even trying to scream made no sound come out. Nick reached down and grabbed Rick's shirt, a tank top, and violently attempted to pull him off the floor with it. The shirt ripped completely in half, and since he was a few feet in the air, he fell out of it and back down to the floor. Nick stood there, stunned that the shirt ripped, while Rick managed to get up off the floor, grab his keys, and run out the door to the car. Rick's story was just hanging there in the air, and none of us moved.

"I went back," he said, a tear in the corner of his eye. "I went back because he asked me to. He apologized and said it would never happen again. You never think that you're going to end up in a situation like that, like domestic abuse is something that always happens to women and is carried out by some redneck named Bubba who's had too much beer. And then there I was going back because he apologized and told me he loved me. I got a real understanding of abuse from being with him, of actually believing that you are nothing without the one that is keeping you within an inch of your life."

He looked directly at Stephen, who was staring, dumbfounded, at both of us.

"Don't go back," Rick said. "You're going to get yourself together and then you deserve better. You shouldn't try a new relationship while you are in recovery, anyway. Every gay person knows that."

He smiled, and I put my hand on his shoulder. I felt like we were parents counseling our wayward kid.

"I really like the person, though," Stephen broke the silence. "He's not a bad person."

"Not a bad person, you're right," said Rick. "But he has a bad habit that masks all that. He won't get help, but you will."

"I'm not sure if I can be on my own," Stephen said.

"Of course you can," I said. "It just doesn't seem like it. The day of Ayers' funeral, I literally slid down the wall in the shower, too emotional to even cry, and I remember thinking that there was no way I could go on. I was hoping I would die of a stroke or something right there in the shower, at my mom's house no less. I remember thinking that the world could not possibly turn for me, that I would be one of those people who walks around shell-shocked for the rest of my life."

Stephen was truly listening, and not, for once, trying to think of a smart comeback.

"But you know what?" I went on. "The world kept turning. Just because he died did not mean it was all going to come to a stop. And it didn't. And I'm here today telling you this story like I should be telling it to Oprah."

Rick and Stephen both smiled at this comment and I knew we had made some ground.

"Okay," Stephen said. "I'll do my best. Can I count on you guys?"

"Yup," I replied easily, knowing that codependence was not a healthy trait, but that it seemed to be part of the gay gene.

An orderly came into the room, telling us that we had to go and that the visitor schedule for Stephen would be determined after his evaluation. As Rick and I walked down the pristine corridors of the recovery center, he put his arm around me, softly singing *Zing Went the Strings of My Heart* in my ear. I knew yet again that I wanted him and all of his self-identified baggage, too. When a thought like this popped in my head, obviously from deep down inside, it could not take long for my mind to begin throwing the "what ifs", to begin reminding me of all the things that could go wrong. I tried to tell myself that it was time to go with it; to focus on what was going on right then and not what may or may not happen in the future. I hoped at that moment that it would not take long for my overactive mind to get the message.

CHAPTER 18

▼

MOMENTS OF TRUTH

I got a phone call from the health center while I was at work, my cell ringer scaring the hell out of me because I thought it was turned off. They asked me to come in. I was so shocked and scared that I just agreed and hung up. My doctor had never asked me to come in, so, after five minutes, I was convinced that my test came up positive. Then Stuart called.

"Those bitches," he said without a hello. "Those bitches at the center don't give any information over the phone anymore. Something about a damned health privacy something or other. What kind of bitch-ass shit is that?"

I was able to calm down upon hearing that news, learning that my HIV blood test phone call equation was no longer valid. Stuart and I made the same arrangements we made the day we had the tests, my plans to go to the gym disappearing in an imaginary splash of tequila and lime, along with a vision of myself twenty pounds heavier. I always assumed that the days I took off from working out would cause me to get fat and loose my figure, as if a couple of days would make a huge difference, just another one of my peculiarities. As I sat at my desk I became scared as I usually did at moments like these, knowing deep down inside that everything would be fine but fighting every nagging fear hanging out in the front of my mind. What if my test was positive and Rick decided he didn't want another positive guy? What if two positives made bad luck? What if Rick got mad if I told him I tested negative? What if I was *happy* about testing negative and that made Rick mad? I hardly got any work done and was obviously distracted, so Madison stopped in my office to find out what was going on.

"What's your problem today?" she asked, hands on the hips of her gray pin-striped pantsuit.

"Just busy, that's all," I lied, obviously.

"Bullshit!" Madison replied. "What's going on?"

"Stuart and I," I said, knowing that it would come out one way or the other, "got HIV tests together at the health center, and now they won't give results over the phone so they called us back in. I always thought that a call to come back in meant bad news, but apparently they just call everybody back in now. We're freaking out, basically."

"You, I don't worry about," she said pointedly, "because you're such a hypochondriac, but Stuart, I worry about him. I'm not even sure he's had a test."

"He hadn't," I said, knowing that Madison would have been able to pin down one of us for the truth anyway. "This was the first."

"It was really sweet of you to go with him, you know," she said, "but maybe I should come too, just in case it's bad news."

"I don't think …" I said, but Madison had already pulled her super-thin cell phone out of her pocket and dialed Stuart.

"I know about the whole blood test bit," she said, "and I'm coming with you. When are you going? Okay. No use arguing, Stuey-boy. What if you needed me? Fine. Goodbye."

I looked at her as I always did at times like this, the all-powerful yet still young and sexy earth mother, keeping us from losing our minds.

"Let me know before you leave," Madison instructed. "Did you think that I would actually let you two get away with this? I didn't think so."

Stuart picked us up at my place and we all piled in the S.S. McGuire to take the short trip to the health center. Madison, playing therapist again, managed to get more truth out of us.

"Don't you two dumb-asses think about these things?" she asked.

"All the time," Stuart lied, while I nodded in agreement.

"I'd be scared, too," she said, knowing how we both felt without much of an explanation.

"So, let's say you were really interested in somebody, well, more than that, let's say you really, really liked a guy and you had to tell him you had it. When would you tell him?"

I had flashbacks to the restaurant with Rick, to all the time we had spent together since then, and to the short time we spent together before then. He had decided to get it out in the open when things could still go south, while not getting together would hurt, but not so bad. I had to admire him for that move, a move I didn't even think about until that moment in the car with Madison and Stuart.

"I think I would wait until we were ready to have sex," Stuart replied, "because then they would have the chance to back out on me if they wanted to."

"When has HIV stopped any of us from having sex with a hottie?" I asked, knowing that it was stopping me lately.

"I don't think I've ever asked," Stuart admitted.

"No," I said. "You know when you're totally connecting with someone. The time to tell would be when you know it could get hot and heavy. Some of us are more careful about having sex with someone when we really like them, anyway."

Neither of them could respond, so we were silent for a whole block. When we got to the health center, we went through the same routine, signing in, sitting, waiting, but this time there was no conversation. Every time Lynnette appeared, Stuart grimaced and Madison patted his hand like an old grandmother. When she finally appeared for us, all she did was wave us inside.

"How could I forget you two?" Lynnette asked. "And who's this?"

"Moral support," Stuart said with a fake smile.

"You gay guys," she said. "You gotta travel in packs and bring your women to the clinic. You know, straight men would be like that if they could. You're all a bunch of babies if you ask me, you gay ones and the straight ones. I got one of each at home, so don't look at me like I don't know what I'm talkin' about."

When we sat down, Madison just stood behind us. Stuart looked pale again, which obviously alarmed nurse Lynnette.

"Don't faint on me again, big boy," she said. "Both of your tests were negative."

There was a collective breathing out from our little group, and I immediately thought about Rick again. I would have to tell him about this adventure.

"Boys," Lynnette said, "I'm concerned about the number of partners you both reported. Please make sure you are taking precautions against HIV and any other diseases. Tell all of your friends, infection rates are on the rise again, so there is concrete evidence that gay men are not protecting themselves. The young ones have the attitude that they are going to get it anyway, the old ones on Viagra are screwin' everything, and some of them now want to keep it on the down low from their girlfriends. Do your part, boys, please. Now get on out of here, and I expect to see you again in six months or so."

Lynnette looked at Madison and said, "Take care of your boys, honey."

"Yes ma'am," replied Madison, with a dainty salute.

We didn't talk on the way home, and I was just looking forward to seeing Rick, although I had been seeing him every day. I had Stuart drop me off at Rick's staircase where I bounded up the stairs to knock on his door. He opened it, pulled me in and gave me a big hug, kissing the top of my head. When he let me go, I saw that he was wearing sweats, white socks, and a t-shirt that had the image of a dollar bill across the bottom and the words, "Atlanta: All you can eat under a dollar." He looked tired, so I spoke first.

"Sorry to just drop in," I said. "You look tired. Are you okay?"

"I am so glad to see you," he said. "I just had one of those bad days, you know? One of those days where I think too much the night before and then drag through it with the same thoughts as the night before."

"That made no sense," I said, tapping him on the forehead.

He grabbed me again, this time kissing me forcefully, his tongue parting my lips so that I could taste his afternoon coffee.

"What's up with you?" he asked. "Besides below the belt there. You know you can't hide the fact that I turn you on."

"Well," I said, deciding to put it out there without thinking through it again, "I went with Stuart to the health clinic and we got HIV tests."

"Good," he said. "And?"

"They were both negative," I reported, waiting for him to feel bad.

"I'm glad to hear that," he said. "More people should be as responsible. You know infection rates are going up again, right?"

"I know," I said, reporting fragments of Lynnette's warnings to us.

"I wasn't sure," I said, "how you would feel about me being negative again."

"What do you mean?" Rick asked, in a sharp tone that startled me.

"I don't know," I said. "I just don't want to celebrate because you have it and you will always have it."

"Baby," he said, "we have to be open about this stuff if we're gonna to make this work. How about if I tell you about my last blood test, then you won't feel so bad."

He led me into the guest bedroom, where he pulled a file from the desk labeled "med". He pulled out a blood test report and went through it methodically, pointing out the important parts.

"See?" he said, pointing at "helper cells". "These are my helpers, or t-cells, which tell us if the immune system is functioning properly. A normal person has t-cells ranging from 800 to in the thousands, and mine are 1100. That's good.

And my viral load, see, is 10,000, which is really great for someone who's not on medication. So, it's all good right now."

"Well," I said, "when do you panic?"

"We don't panic anymore," Rick said, "because the doctor looks for trends in your counts, like are the t-cells headed steadily down and is the viral load headed steadily up. If so, we've planned to look at medications. We'll cross that bridge when we come to it, huh?"

"All right," I said, amazed again at Rick's confidence and knowledge.

"I'll go with you the next time you get tested," he said, "but I'm seriously hoping we get to have sex before then."

Rick smiled when he said this, that sly smile that made me weak in the knees. I still did not feel ready to have sex with him, although I was beginning to feel totally turned on again. I had feelings for him that came through loud and clear at that moment, a sober moment, versus the night in the closet at Stephen's house, feelings that I knew I could no longer avoid. Instead of pushing us apart, my own responsibility for the HIV test was bringing us closer, a ridiculously small thing in comparison to the world around us, but a huge thing in this little world we were creating for ourselves. Rick had his hands on my shoulders, looking down at me, his eyes bright with anticipation, giving off the sense that he knew I would not be able to say no to him much longer.

"Let's get a pizza," he said. "I'm starving. Let's get one of those white pizzas from that place on Cooper, you know, where they have that great Chianti and the little tables in the windows?"

"Sounds great," I said. "I'm glad I came by."

"Me too," he said, smiling again.

CHAPTER 19

▼

COMING CLEAN

A few days later, I had dinner at Rick's apartment. The arrangement was starting to make us both wonder exactly what was happening between the two of us. I was very aware of my feelings for Rick, feelings that I had not felt since I met Ayers. I had always been ready for immediate action or gratification, depending on the situation. If someone gave me a box of chocolates, I would usually eat the whole box right away, so there was no slow savor to anything I did. I was being forced into slow action because of my own feelings and irrational fears, something that I was not comfortable with and definitely not accustomed to. Those feelings for Rick were already too strong to back out, even while I was still trying to convince myself that this was the right thing to do. I worried every night about the fear that Rick would go cold on me or change his mind because I was taking so long to decide where our relationship stood. Neither of us wanted to admit how strange it really was, the fact that the only thing missing at this point was the physical side of the relationship, because I had the idea that gay guys, ourselves included, always seemed to make the move to the physical at supersonic speed, leaving the straight people just kissing at the doorway after a hot date. I tried to think of it from some other guy's perspective, from the perspective of someone who may not have been through what I'd been through. I came to the conclusion that if the ordinary thirty-something gay guy on the street had the chance with Rick, he would probably jump at it. Rick was, in spite of the one imperfection, quite a catch, smart, funny, educated, well-employed, and hot as hell. I wondered why I would refer to HIV as an imperfection, like a diamond would have a flaw or the designer shirt you just picked off the rack at the Last Call outlet had a bad stitch in it. I began to think that maybe I was making too big of a deal about the whole situation, but it was never my nature to be completely worry-free. I had to think through every situation heavily before I could sleep over it at night. I decided to bring it up again, to make sure Rick was aware that I was still confused but definitely into him. How many more conversations like this would he be willing to go through?

When I arrived for dinner Rick answered the door in camouflage shorts, the kind that let his calves peek out at the bottom, and a black ribbed tank top. He was bulging out of both, so I was immediately tongue-tied.

"What's up?" he asked, as he dished out linguine with meat sauce.

"I'm just so stupid," I replied. "I'm just not able to think about anything rationally anymore."

"Alex, you're not stupid. You're scared," he pointed out. "I think I would be, too, but there's really no middle ground here. It's all or nothing."

This explicit warning startled me. Rick stopped messing with the food and took me by the shoulders to turn me toward him. I thought he was going to kiss me, but instead looked right in my eyes in a way that I had not seen before.

"I happen to have fallen in love with you," he said slowly, "and now I'm the one that's afraid of getting hurt. Maybe you're making too much out of this. If you change your mind, I'm not sure I can deal. I don't need another friend, Alex. I need a partner and stability. You may be willing to be alone to save yourself from pain but I'm not. How far are you going to go to ensure that you never get hurt again? It's a promise that you just can't make to yourself. If you love again, I can guarantee you will hurt at some point or another."

I was stunned, like he had just pulled my plug. I couldn't think of anything to say.

"Maybe you need to stay away to make up your mind," he stated coldly, "because your mind may think you can have your cake and eat it too. I mean, look at us, we're practically doing everything together except that one important thing that you just can't bring yourself to get into. You *are* thinking about this way too much, and it's time to piss or get off the pot, Alex."

I was looking at my feet, staring at my ridiculous Prada sandals while realizing that Rick had just nailed me head on, as if I had a target right in the middle of my chest.

"You should at least stay for the linguine," he said, "because otherwise I'll have to eat it for the next week and a half. Come on, sit down."

I sat, obediently.

"You know," he said, "I can't resist you, which is my own stupid problem. I don't want to send you away because I want to be with you. I just think maybe you could stand to be alone for a few days to work this out."

I again did not answer, knowing that he was probably right. Just then my cell phone rang. Stephen was calling from the recovery center.

"I talked to Nick yesterday," he reported. "I told him that I just can't be involved with him right now. Thanks for helping me."

"What was Nick's reaction?" I asked.

"He acted like he really didn't care," Stephen replied. "And I was trying to go by the book, man. I'm really sad about it, but hell, there's other things going on here."

"Like what?" I asked, not really wanting to know but imagining it all the same.

"Oh, stuff," he answered. "There are ways to sneak off and have a little somethin' somethin', you know?"

"Somethin' what?" I inquired, wondering if people in the rehab were actually still doing drugs.

"Sex," Stephen said. "We can sneak off for sex. There's this guy down the hall and, well …"

"Okay, okay," I said. "I get it."

I had hoped that they handled all addictions there, but apparently the recovery center was not aware that sex addiction was rampant. I had mixed emotions. On one hand, if he was having sex then maybe he would crave a cigarette or a chocolate bar instead of the drugs, but on the other hand, sex could be a gateway to the drugs, too. All I could do was hope that this was right for Stephen.

I reported the entire conversation to Rick, who appeared worried about the fact that Stephen pegged us both as the reasons he changed his mind about Nick. Rick and I ate linguine in silence, or in as much silence as an Italian can eat linguine. Rick kept offering me red wine, but I refused, knowing that alcohol was probably a bad idea at the time. I finally broke the silence.

"How did you find out?" I asked. "About being positive?"

"Well," Rick explained, "after the mistake I made, I got tested every three months or so. It happened only a couple of months before I met Nick."

"Exactly what happened?" I asked, not caring if it was insensitive.

Rick paused for a second and looked at me curiously, as if he was trying to decide if it was even worth it to explain.

"Is it worth it to explain, Elizabeth?" he asked, using one of the famous couple nicknames we had bestowed on each other.

I shrugged and loaded up another mouthful of linguine. I was hungry and didn't want to be the one doing the talking.

Rick made friends with a guy at the family business, Kenny, so they started hanging out together, he explained. There was no pretense in the sexual orientation department, both of them talking openly about being gay. Kenny was not ugly but not stunning either, and had a very fine-tuned ability to smooth talk anyone, from the admins in the business to the sandwich lady at the supermarket, who always slipped him extra meat and cheese for free. On one of their frequent Saturday night outings, Rick and Kenny went to a club, and after some heavy drinking, Kenny began to hit on Rick very aggressively. Rick had not seen this side of Kenny, but found himself eyeing him in a different way, the way of wondering what he looked like naked or what sex with him would be like. Rick laughed it off, he explained, as being drunk and also to the fact that he felt he could trust Kenny. At one point Rick got up to go the bathroom, leaving Kenny at the bar. In the bathroom, Rick ran into a few people he knew and ended up chatting with them for a few minutes. I stopped eating and was listening intently. The tone of Rick's voice told me there was more to this story than just a simple mistake.

When Rick went back to the bar, Kenny was still sitting there so he apologized for taking so long and finished his drink. Rick recalled thinking that the last drink got him really drunk, drunk enough to not be overly concerned about what was going on. Kenny was still coming on very strong, so Rick just went with it and agreed to go back to his place. It was one of those actions that was known to be wrong to the person doing it but the allure of a decadent act was stronger than any other feeling. Rick never made the assumption that Kenny may have put something in his drink, so he thought he was in control up to a certain point. His rationalization was that he could have sex with a guy he knew and that could be the end of it, or it could be the start of a "friends with benefits" arrangement. The two went back to Kenny's apartment where Rick remembered clearly the act of getting naked, the act of becoming amused at the fact that Kenny had a really good body that was cleverly hidden under dumpy clothes, but that was about it. Rick woke up the next day and knew that he had had a lot of sex during the night, so he left awkwardly. Kenny quit the business soon after and Rick did not hear from him for weeks, until Kenny called to tell him that he had tested positive. When Rick did not show as much concern as Kenny thought he should, Kenny reminded him that they had not used condoms, to which Rick became very angry. Kenny also reminded him that he was pretty much a little slut that night, that he had agreed to bareback sex without any hesitation. Rick knew that this behavior was not normal for him, and that he would not have consented to this activity, even in a state of drunkenness. He stayed ashamed for becoming a statistic that the entire community had been warned against repeatedly. Rick's voice trailed off and as he looked at me I got up and put my arms around his shoulders. I just listened to someone bare his soul about how his life changed, and he wasn't even completely responsible.

"Shit," he said. "That was embarrassing. I just told you I trusted the wrong person, who probably put a date rape drug in my drink and infected me with the thing that changed my life forever. That's another situation you never think you're going to end up in."

"When did Nick come into the picture?" I asked, not wanting to rub salt in the wound but wanting to get it all out in the open.

"Nick ..." he paused for a second before he started the story. "Nick wandered into one of our shops while I was there. It was just a few weeks after the whole Kenny thing. We started talking and that was about it—you know Nick is pretty hot, and that smile—well, that did it. I'm not sure if I was desperate or what, but I think there was a part of him that I really thought I could love, one good spot in him, you know, until that good spot was hidden by all the bad in him."

Rick pushed back from the table and drank down more wine. He usually sipped wine, so his noisy gulping made me more nervous than I already was.

"Thinking about the fact that I could test positive at any time impaired my judgment. Here I was, feeling like used goods, like no one would ever want me again, especially if they knew how I'd gotten HIV, but with a hottie like Nick after me. We didn't even really date, we sort of started doing couple things right away. There was no romance, no soft shoe wooing, just right to the business of coupling. We really didn't even have sex that much ..."

He paused again, as if he were getting up the courage to finish. I watched as his usually confident eyes betrayed him. He and Nick moved in together, but Rick did not tell him about what happened with Kenny. He just kept getting tested every three months, barely breathing while he waited for the results. Rick said he knew when the test would come back positive, that he had a sort of premonition of it, and when it did he was not shocked or in denial. He just moved to deal with it.

"So," he continued, "I explained the whole thing and told Nick. He got really mad, throwing things, yelling and screaming, accusing me of cheating, but that was one time that he didn't come after me. We split up after about six more months. I don't think he ever touched me again. I tried to hang around Atlanta after we broke up, but couldn't. You know the rest of the story."

I could not react to all of this information, so I just put my hand on his. I didn't feel sorry for Rick, I just felt relieved that he had been so honest about the whole story. My attraction for him grew again. I was just about to kiss him when the screeching of car tires and the slamming of a door distracted us.

CHAPTER 20

▼

ANGER

The pounding on the door ruined the moment that was about to occur between Rick and me. He looked up, not quite surprised, and I saw that his eyes were back to their usual confidence level.

"Ever notice," he inquired with a laugh, "that phones and doors are our worst enemies? Something always happens. I'm gonna quit answering either one of them. You may have to start climbing through the window and sending smoke signals. Maybe Morse code ..."

He was talking as he went to the back door, so when I heard him say, "Jesus!" I was startled. Nick pushed past him and into the kitchen, stomping so hard I thought the china was going to fall out of the cabinets. Nick came into the dining room with a nasty look on his face, much worse than his normal bad-boy look. His hair was falling in his face, which was a shade of red I had not seen on a person since Madison's kid held his breath to get her attention.

"What the fuck?" Nick said, quietly but with so much tension that his teeth were gritted. "Why are you two suddenly calling the shots with Stephen? What did you tell him?"

Nick turned to Rick and looked him dead in the eye.

"What did *you* say?" he hissed.

Before Rick could answer, I felt my protective side coming out. Again, the good had to defend the stupid in the gay food chain, although I had really begun to doubt what I perceived as stupidity in Stephen. He lacked good sense but certainly wasn't stupid.

"Nick," I said, so calmly that I wasn't sure I had even said it. "I was the one who told Stephen he should reconsider having a relationship right now. He's in trouble and needs to get his addictions under control."

Nick clinched his fist, first the right one and then the left one. I looked down at myself, in my tight t-shirt, my body flexing its muscles without me really thinking about them, and thought for the first time that I could take care of myself. I was not afraid of this guy and would be able to defend myself if necessary.

"It's none of your fucking business," Nick raised his voice.

I responded just as calmly as I had before. "It *is* my business, Nick. I never loved Stephen, but I do care for him. He's smart, good looking, and really a good guy, so I want to see him succeed. If you care for him as much as you say, maybe you could understand and let him decide the timeframe for when he's ready. Honesty hasn't been one of his strong points so I told him that it would be the best thing."

I thought that if Nick and Stephen did eventually get together, I had pretty much just crossed myself off of their Saturday night bridge list. Rick stood motionless, silent, watching me take responsibility, even though he was there when we had the conversation with Stephen. I was happy with his silence.

"Honesty?" Nick asked, his jaw finally slacking enough to make the redness go out of his face. "Ask your boyfriend here about honesty. Did he tell you what happened? Did he tell you the whole story of how he ended up here?"

The subject changed so quickly that I began to question Nick's motive for being there. Rick shifted on his feet nervously, looked at me, and then shot an angry glance at Nick.

"You should stay out of it, Nick," Rick said sharply.

"Why?" Nick snapped. "You guys are all brave and everything, like you want to save Stephen, so maybe I want to be a good guy and save Alex."

Nick looked at me, again so coldly, like there was no soul behind his eyes at all. I was preparing myself for some major revelation, a huge deal breaker that would send me packing back to my own little world, the world that existed before Stephen or Rick.

"Your knight in shining armor walked out on *me*," said Nick, in newscaster style, like the next thing out of his mouth would be "film at ten o'clock". He stopped for dramatic effect, but this drama was nearly as bad as my high school production of the Interpreter's Theater.

Nick went on. "I told him that I could deal with the HIV thing and he walked out on me while I was at work. I came home and he left a fucking note that said he was leaving. That was such a shitty way of ending it, like a fucking coward or something."

Nick's voice quivered a tiny bit while he was explaining. Rick looked sheepish, like a dog caught wetting the sofa, and then turned to me.

"It's all go around here tonight, isn't it?" I asked.

"I didn't tell you that part of the story," Rick said, "because I thought you would think I was weak. I had to get out of there."

Rick decided that he had to stand up for himself in a safe way, which was to leave when he wasn't angry. He gathered his clothes, his photos, and a few pieces of art that meant something to him and put them in the car. He sat down at the kitchen table and penned out a letter to Nick that explained how he had at one time loved him in some way, that it was the first drops of love that could have changed over time if things had been right between the two of them. At the time he was writing the letter, he knew that this could never have been true, that if you don't know you love someone right away then it probably wouldn't work out anyway, but he kept writing. He wrote about how Nick made him feel like he couldn't live without him, while all along he felt like he couldn't live with Nick. He asserted that he was a person without Nick, he was a person with HIV who had a value in the world and could have a value to someone else. After pouring out his heart, he asked Nick's forgiveness for letting it go as far as it had, and for walking out in that way. The letter came down to Rick explaining to Nick that he was afraid of him, afraid of what he was capable of, and afraid that Nick would kill him before anything else had a chance. With that, he folded the letter, left it on the kitchen table where Nick was sure to leave his keys, and left. Rick's voice trailed off and Nick's eyes closed at the same time, like he was thinking about something that had already happened.

"So why do you find it necessary to beat people up?" I asked Nick, amazed at the balls I had just grown. "I mean, does that make you feel like a man or something? All I have to do is look down to make myself feel like a man."

Nick clenched a fist again and moved toward me. I puffed out my chest as he took his flat left hand and shoved me against the wall with it. I swung, fist closed, for the first time in my entire life. The few fights I had been in over the years were usually ended by me throwing something, like rocks or other inanimate objects. When my fist made contact with Nick's jaw, he fell against the table, taking a few dirty dishes with him. It happened so fast that he just didn't see it coming, and I nearly wet my pants immediately after he fell because I really thought he was going to kill me. Rick jumped over to Nick, lying in the floor with his hand in a half-eaten pile of linguine, and put his hand over Nick's chest, as if he were trying to stop him from getting up. I was so angry by that time that I started screaming, the captive energy caused by all of the drama, from Stephen to Nick to Rick to HIV and back to my own indecision cascading out of me like I was being exorcized.

"Do you want more?" I shouted. "Do you want to fight me, you goddamned asshole faggot? Do you want me to kick your fucking ass, you tit sucking freak?"

I was gasping for air after this tirade, not even recognizing the stream of obscenity coming from my mouth as my own, watching Nick and Rick staring at me like I had three heads. Nick pushed himself back on his elbows, scooting through the garbage on the floor, seemingly trying to get away from both of us.

"Um, Alex?" Rick said softly.

"What?" I shrieked back. "What, goddamit?"

I had not been this angry since Ayers died, when I reached that stage my shrink called "anger". I spent weeks screaming at my mother over the phone, screaming at Stuart in person, and screaming at the shrink. My eyes started to sting as I broke my mother's rule number one and stormed out, hearing Rick's voice, at first in his apartment, then at the back door as I headed down the stairs. I wasn't sure what he was saying, my ears were buzzing with so many voices. I got in my car, screeched into reverse, and jolted out onto the street, much too angry to be driving but with nowhere else to go to get away.

My cell was ringing but I couldn't answer it. The CD player was going but I wasn't listening. My thoughts were going a mile a minute, not sure who I was mad at or if I was mad at myself or even mad at my mother for teaching me to keep my feelings to myself. I ended up somewhere between midtown and downtown Memphis, cruising past the gay bars and empty office buildings. I came to an intersection, a fairly familiar one, and stopped at the red light, the first car in the line, ready to scratch off again as soon as the light turned green. For some reason, I felt as if taking life off of the already expensive tires on the BMW was some sort of general retribution on the world. When the light turned green, I floored it.

I didn't see the minivan coming from my right, on the passenger side, running the red light. The impact started a shower of metal and broken glass as my head snapped to the left, hitting the window. I heard the screeching of rubber, the cracking of glass, the twisting of metal, and the rushing sound of liquids being ejected from their containers, sounds that are very foreign and not something one hears every day. By the time the driver of the car crossing the intersection in the opposite direction noticed what was happening, it was too late.

My car was spun again, this time from an impact to the left front, while still impaled on what I found out later was a 1998 Dodge Caravan. I could feel the front of the car coming into the passenger compartment, the frame bending and screeching again, the glass in the door on my side of the car finally giving way and showering all over me. For a split second I recognized that my blood was running down my face, until the pain in my legs made me shout out. When this mass of three cars came to rest, my right arm was trapped grotesquely between the center console and the passenger seat and my left leg was painfully caught in the wreckage at my feet. Fragmented glass was all over me, even stuck in the torrent of blood that was erupting from the cuts on my head and face. The van was somehow at the side of my car, and the big car that was traveling in the opposite direction had come to rest somewhere beyond the intersection. I saw concerned faces with cell phones, arms gesturing, people talking at me through the broken glass and the hissing of car parts and the wheezing of the airbags, before I finally slumped forward in a puff of powder.

I woke up again as I was being lifted out of the car, a great big burly fireman having grasped me securely under the arms to pull me out. I tried to move my right arm but it wouldn't budge, and my left leg was hanging limply, being dragged over what used to be the leather top of the car. A totally hot EMT was suddenly looking down at me as I was placed on a stretcher, asking me to grab his fingers with my left hand.

"Does he have a cell phone?" I heard someone ask, then felt the hands going through my pockets, where I had indeed left the phone. I knew that I had no identification on me, my wallet left on my dresser in my haste to get over to Rick's for dinner. I was suddenly aware of a terrible pain in my side, also on the left, as hottie EMT pulled up my shirt and then sliced it with his scissors in one quick move. I was conscious enough at the moment to curse the EMT for cutting up my brand new t-shirt. He was talking to me again, but it sounded like he was at the end of a tunnel.

"Rick!" I thought to myself, and then everything went black again.

The next time I was conscious, I was in the emergency room, with braces on my left leg and my right arm, drunk and groggy on whatever medication they gave me. I tried to sit up and saw Rick at the end of the bed talking to a man I assumed was the doctor. I caught pieces of the conversation as I wandered in and out of a woozy wakened state.

"… said it was lucky that you had called his cell phone or else they wouldn't have known to call anyone …"

"... broken in two places, could need surgery but we need to do some x-rays ..."

"... afraid he had a punctured lung but it just looks like he's pretty bruised up on that side ..."

"... he'll be fine but it will take a while to heal ... pretty drugged up right now ..."

Then I heard Rick's voice. "I'll be here ... not going anywhere ..."

I felt Rick's hand on my arm as I fell into a blissfully ignorant, drugged-out sleep.

Chapter 21

▼

Trying to Float

When I was about three, my parents took my brother and me to a friend's house to enjoy the swimming pool. I apparently got a kick out of floating on a raft that had a little picture window in it, my attention drawn to the funny shapes in the water. I couldn't quite handle the water yet, as opposed to my brother, who might as well have been born with gills. At the age of four, he was swimming like a porpoise while his little brother was a solid landlubber.

I'm not sure how I fell off that raft, but I remember looking up at the surface of the water and the raft I had just vacated. A three year old with no inclination to water sinks like a stone, and that is just what I did. My brother saw this, dove in, and grabbed me by the arm, pulling my little body up to the surface and out of the water. I don't remember anything else about this incident, just the raft and what it looked like from the bottom. The sensation of the beginning stages of drowning stayed with me over the years, the idea that you want to reach up and grab the surface of the water in hopes that it will hold you up enough to get your nose and mouth into the fresh air. I was afraid of the water from that point on, even when the evil swimming teacher my mother insisted on sending us to pushed my face into the water without so much as a warning.

The night of the accident, I went in and out of that weird drugged state, although Rick and the doctor assured me that at no point was I near death. I remember that trying to make myself conscious was like my near drowning, an attempt to grab hold of something that couldn't support me. Every time I wanted to say something or ask questions, I saw Rick's or a nurse's face and I couldn't hold on, just sank back to the bottom of my consciousness. In this veil of drugs and pain I thought about how that near-drowning way back in 1975 made me afraid of everything, from water to thunderstorms to the little harmless dog named Bitsy on our street. My father even offered me twenty dollars to pet Bitsy, but I turned down the money when I saw the little monster chasing our neighbors, the Kleins, in their big wood paneled station wagon. I somehow made fear the decision maker throughout my life, fear keeping me from pursuing many of the things I wanted to pursue. It was the easy route I had taken until Ayers and his illness changed my life. Amid the sounds of the hospital that night, ringing phones, chattering voices, the occasional ambulance siren, I wandered around in my thoughts feeling that I had adapted a no-fear attitude. As the drugs wore off, I knew that the no-fear attitude was suited to my needs and not anyone else's, and certainly not to the needs of two together. I was afraid of losing Rick, of going through illness, of having to watch him lose his independence, and afraid of anything in general that would take me out of the safe box I had built for myself over the past three years. Being T-boned by a minivan and run over by a land barge at the same time made me conscious of the fact that life could not be lived in a box, that risk was part of life, and love by itself was a risk even if it was not punctuated by a disease that was manageable but not curable.

As I woke up the next day, I hoped that the accident had banged the fear out of me, but as I became aware of my situation, I knew I had a few more things to deal with before dealing with the fear. There was a cast on my left leg, all the way up to my knee. It seemed to be holding some nail biting pain. My right arm was in a cast and in a sling, also throbbing with pain. I was aware of bandages on my head, hanging over my left eye, as well as an IV in my good arm, along with a wrap around my midsection that was probably tighter than the best whalebone girdle.

"What a mess," I murmured, also becoming aware of the fact that the hospital gown was the only thing covering up my nakedness.

"Thank God," Rick's voice said from the direction of a bright light. "You're finally making some sense."

I turned slightly and saw him stepping over from the window, a hopeful expression on his face, a cup of coffee in his hand.

"Am I dead?" I said stupidly through the haze, and then continued in song, "is that all there is? If that's all there is, my friends ..."

"I spoke too soon," said Rick, sitting down in the chair next to the bed, placing his warm hands on my forehead. "Anyway, you're not dead yet." He said this in his sly way, playing on my dramatic hypochondria.

"Okay, give me the bad news," I muttered again, not sure really what I was saying. "How long have I got?"

"If you keep eating so much cheese and drinking hard liquor," Rick said seriously, "probably not another 40 years." Then he softened. "You dope. You're fine. I'm afraid the news is not good for the drama queen in you, though. Sorry to say you didn't have a near-death experience. You're pretty banged up. I was worried until I got to see you."

My head started to clear a little more, still fuzzy about the events of the night before, but knowing that I had decked Nick with one shot.

"I'm sorry," I said softly. "I'm sorry I caused all of this trouble. Is Nick hurt?"

"Just his pride," Rick said, and then chuckled with a fake feminine lisp. "You were magnifithent. My hero!"

"Cut it out," I said, with a weak smile. "What's going on with me, then?"

"First," Rick said, "you're lucky I was able to flirt with the doctor so he would tell me what's happening. I told him you were an orphan after your celebrity parents were killed in a plane crash that had something to do with a freebasing incident."

"Oh, ha, ha," I remarked, knowing that I would need to call my parents in Mississippi as soon as I could handle a conversation with them.

Rick explained that I had multiple injuries that would appear to be more of an inconvenience than anything else. My left leg had a very simple but painful hairline fracture, just below the knee, an amazingly small injury based on the amount of damage to the car. My right arm was also broken, again cleanly, from being trapped momentarily between the console and the seat, which also dislocated my shoulder, the reason I was stuck in the sling. When my body reacted to the impact on the driver's side, the door handle and the inside panel rammed me securely in the ribs on my left side, starting below my armpit and ending right before there could have been major internal damage, leaving a great deal of soreness and the possibility of cracked ribs. My head had bounced around pretty badly between the two impacts, and to top it all off, I had assorted cuts on my head, face, and arms from flying glass. Luckily there was no glass in my eyes but there was a pretty deep gash on the left side of my forehead that would probably leave a scar.

"There is a little more bad news," he went on. "Dr. Whatsit says that someone is going to have to watch you for the next three days, but they are not going to keep you here. The other bad news is that the nurse would positively not allow me to give you a sponge bath, so you may be a little stinky. I was hoping to get a peek."

"Ugh," I grunted.

"But wait," Rick said in an infomercial voice, "there's more! He says you may have some trouble doing things for yourself while you have the casts and the sling. He also said you may have some memory problems from the concussion, in which case you are my sex slave and we do it twelve times each day."

"Oh great," I said. "What am I gonna do? I just can't handle my mother helping me to the bathroom."

"Don't worry about it," Rick said. "Everything is under control. Madison is going to take care of stuff at the office and I am going to hang around to make sure you don't take a poop on your sofa."

I started to protest but Rick put his hand up, touching my lips lightly. When he sat back down, a fly landed on my face, a scary thing that a dirty insect could be inside the hospital. I began to fidget, trying to blow the fly off, and when I tried to bring my right arm up to swat, the pain in my side caused me to gasp and then groan. The fly took off, but ended up back on my face as Rick sat reading the latest issue of *Vanity Fair*. I flailed again, realizing that I was not really a whole person right then, and finally Rick looked up from his magazine and shooed the fly away. I rolled my eyes, the look that he had become intimately familiar with, as he sat down on the bed and rubbed my shoulder. I was not very independent at that point, but I assumed that this condition would get better after I was released from the hospital.

"Was anybody else hurt?" I asked, expecting the worst.

"Just minor injuries, apparently," he said, "but your car is toast."

I had not thought about the car until that moment. The BMW was one of the biggest indulgences in my life, purchased as a reminder of when I finally arrived in my career, making more money than necessary to live. I thought briefly about my Italian grandfather who screamed about the fact that my mom's 1984 Oldsmobile had an automatic antenna that went up and down when the radio was turned on and off. I was the first person in my family to purchase a luxury sports car, and most of my relatives criticized me for it. That BMW was a symbol of the fact that I chose to be different from all of my family members.

"Another sign," I whispered. "Time to make changes."

My voice trailed off again as I fell once again into a sleep. I could still feel Rick's hand on me, his presence that invisible thing that I could grab to stay afloat. Maybe there was nothing left to be afraid of.

CHAPTER 22

▼

ACCEPTING HELP

Rick helped me into the wheelchair as the impatient yet ample orderly waited to push me out to the car. I had the cast on my left leg and the sling and cast on my right arm, and was still very lightheaded from taking so much pain medication. I was not accustomed to the lack of balance, presence of mind, and even the simple ability to stand without the fear of going back down again. When I stood up the first time, I slid back down on the bed, the only time I had seen Rick look alarmed. Ms. Orderly chomped her gum once more, reached around the front of me, and dragged me all the way back onto the bed. They stood there looking at me like I was going to do the can-can, and I really got irritated.

"Stop staring at me," I blurted. "Both of you. I'm gonna try this on my own if it kills me."

"Okay, honey," smacked Ms. Orderly, "just be careful. I don't wanna have to sponge your ass again. I'm leavin' that to your boyfriend here."

I glared at her, hard enough to make her chew the gum with her mouth closed, and stood again. I stomped around the room a couple of times, making the bad leg scream in pain and the good one scream from being used so much. When I tried to sit in the chair next to the bed, I again lost my balance and fell backwards. Then I couldn't get up. Rick held out his hand, bent his knees, and helped me come up to a standing position.

"Alex," he said evenly, "you're just going to have to let me help you for two weeks. That's how long the doctor said the cast would stay on, then you can use a brace. You'll be stronger then. I know you don't like it, but for Christ's sake just accept the help and keep on steppin'."

Even in my cranky state, his comment made me smile. I obediently let him help me back into the wheelchair and gave a crisp command for Ms. Orderly to get her bleached blonde ass in gear. I waited for Rick at the entrance of the hospital and smiled again when I saw him drive up. His car always looked like it had just driven out of the Audi showroom, detail fresh, and he looked absolutely gorgeous behind the wheel of it.

He jumped out, came around to my side, and smoothly helped me into the front seat, pushed back far enough to accommodate my left leg, which had to remain stretched out in front of me. I was so jumpy on the ride home that Rick kept asking me if I was going to make it. Every intersection was a terror and I was afraid that there was a monster minivan waiting just on the other side to T-bone me again. My brake foot was on the good leg, so I made an unconscious show of pumping the imaginary brake, much to Rick's annoyance.

After the fifth time, he spoke up. "Just cut it out, will you?" he snapped. "You're making me crazy with your drivers ed teacher moves over there. Close your eyes or something. I should have given you another pain pill before we left."

"Sorry," I replied. "I'm a tiny bit nervous."

"Really?" he said sarcastically. "A stripper on a Navy destroyer would be less nervous."

Rick pulled the car up to my staircase, glanced up, and then looked back at me. We both laughed loud wondering how in the hell we would get me up three flights of stairs without a tantrum. He came around to my side of the car and again helped me go upright.

"Just put the stiff one out to the side and I'll go up next to you," he instructed, and then added, "Damn, I haven't heard anybody say that in a few years."

"Vintage is in," I said. "Elevators are out, according to my queer real estate agent. Elevators are only out if you don't need one."

I hopped up one flight of the wrought iron staircase and came to rest on the first landing, huffing and puffing with the first beads of sweat coming off my forehead. During the summer, in the Southern humidity, I would sweat before I set foot out the door. Now I was working really hard and still worried about what Rick thought of me. My right leg started to spasm as if I had just done a few heavy sets of squats at the gym. At least there I could have grunted with only a few funny looks.

By the second landing, I could see we were both getting annoyed, not at each other, but at the seemingly endless trek up to my apartment. It did have a great view of the park through the beveled glass windows, a view that I enjoyed even more after that day. I stood there, not knowing if I could even make it. Rick pushed in front of me, squatted down, and turned his head back toward me.

"Hop on," he said. "It's only a few more."

"Good God," I laughed. "You'll screw your back up for sure if you try to lift me."

"Trust me," he said seriously, and suddenly, completely, for the first time, I did.

When we got into my place, I settled onto the sofa with a cold Frappucino in a bottle fresh from the fridge, and the *New York Times*. Rick, assured that I would survive for a while on my own, went to park his car and go back to his place, relieved not to hear me bitching in the background for just a few minutes.

By the time I got to the end of the front page, the Frappucino kicked in and I knew I would have to somehow make a trip to the bathroom. I stared at the bathroom door, then back at my stiff leg, and then back at the bathroom door again. I realized that my usual afternoon trip to the toilet was not going to be possible without Rick's assistance, and hoped that I could work out a system to get there by myself within the next two weeks. I picked up my cell and called Rick.

"I have to poop," I whined. "And I can't get there."

Rick laughed really loud, tried to say something, and then laughed again. By the time he hung up, he was already through my back door, coming at me with his arms open. He knelt down in front of me, put his hands on my shoulders, and through his laughter, told me how "freakin' cute" I was. He helped me up again, and stood close while I humped over to the bathroom.

"You are not going to help me get on the pot," I said, "because I just can't deal with that."

"Honey, you've got to give up your pride and realize that we all do it the same way," Rick said, laughing again, "so I'm going to stand near the door just in case. This way I can hear the splash, too."

With that, he started laughing really hard, slapping his thighs and snorting. I did manage a little sarcastic laugh as I slammed the bathroom door. I don't remember how I lowered myself onto the cold toilet seat, but I do remember thinking that Rick just did not care about my bodily functions. We had passed the point where any of it mattered, and I silently cursed the fact that sex was just not a possibility until the slings and casts came off.

Rick made dinner and served it to me on a tray, even placing a little flower from the bushes downstairs in a sherry glass next to my plate. I was finally hungry and tried to eagerly attack my food, a chicken breast with rice and asparagus. I stared at the food until Rick came over apologizing for being so thoughtless.

"Poor baby!" he shouted. "I gave you that big ole piece of chicken and you've only got one good arm! I was still crazy over the whole bathroom thing."

Rick gallantly cut my chicken into bite-sized pieces, even offering to feed them to me, which I briefly considered but then figured it was a little over the top. After dinner, he brought my medications, insisting that he would have to watch me to make sure I took everything I was supposed to take.

It was at that moment that my life changed again, even more so than the accident two days earlier. I watched Rick moving around in my apartment, cooking, cleaning, cutting my food, handing out medication, and even helping me go to the bathroom. The irony of the whole situation hit me harder than the minivan had. I was completely dependent on Rick and he was going right along with it. He was taking care of me, even my basest human need to expel my own waste, when all along my fear was that I would have to do the same for him. He sat by my side in the hospital, running interference with the doctors and nurses, even talking to my mother once or twice during the night. He'd told me a few weeks earlier that his greatest fear was the fear of losing his independence and becoming a burden, and here I was, dependent and certainly a burden. The thought of loss was one thing, something that I had dealt with before, but there was no denying that what I had expected to have to do for Rick was what he was now doing for me. He helped me into bed, after the major spectacle of me trying to get my ripped jeans over the cast without him seeing all of my stuff, and made sure that my cell phone was close enough to reach.

"This reminds me of being sick as a kid," I said, slurring through the muted effects of the painkiller. "My mom would make sure I had everything I needed and then she would leave a little bell so that I could ring for her if I needed her."

I was always prone to strep throat, I explained, and would end up with high fevers that made me slightly delirious. During these mini-deliriums, my mother would come in to my room in her blue velour robe and sit by my bed until I felt better and could go back to sleep. I never had trouble going back to sleep when she was there, sometimes telling me little stories that I never caught the end of. Up to this point, the only time I had been this ill as an adult was in college when I caught a nasty case of mono. As I got sicker and sicker I took a chance and drove from my apartment near campus to my parents' house, which at the time was in the suburbs. My mother took one look at me and put me to bed in the guest bedroom, leaving the little bell just in case I needed something—although I was nearly 22 years old at the time—and chatting quietly to me until I fell asleep. I wondered if there were details like this in Rick's childhood.

"What was your childhood like?" I asked him, dreamily, and then went on, "I should call my mom …"

Rick explained that we could have had identical childhoods, where mom and dad were together and all of the kids went to regular public school and were home for the holidays. Rick's mother even stayed home until he and his sisters were in high school, old enough to let themselves in after school and start their homework. Even though they were financially well off, the Monettes made the kids get jobs if they wanted to have a social life or a car. Rick talked about one particular Christmas when he was not quite too old to believe in Santa, when Christmas was still such a magical time for a kid. When he woke up on Christmas morning, an entire train set was up and running and the tag on the table had his name on it, written in handwriting that was neither his mother's nor his father's.

"Isn't it great," Rick mused, "to have memories like this? Some people just aren't so lucky."

"When did you figure it out?" I asked, referring to the sudden realization of being much different than most of the other boys.

"High school was hell," Rick said quietly, and continued to explain why.

Rick knew for sure in ninth grade, when showering with the other boys after gym class became a struggle to avert his eyes. He didn't have a girlfriend, but hung around with the kids from the yearbook, school paper, and literary society. Rick chuckled as he explained that most of the kids with questionable sexuality ended up in the literary society, scratching out their frustrations through dark poetry and ironic, cynical short stories where the underdog won the day. He was particularly chummy with one such dark poet, Cindy, and together they were a writing team, taking potshots at anybody and anything with their poetry and prose. Everyone thought he and Cindy were together, and after the first high school reunion, he discovered why they had been so chummy when she showed up with her girlfriend. Rick also became close to the illustrator in the literary society, a male version of Cindy. When an after school meeting turned into a make out session, the boy illustrator and Rick became an item that nobody knew about. But when senior prom time came, he explained to his parents that he wasn't going because he had a boyfriend. The Monettes reacted well and invited the illustrator over for dinner immediately.

I'm not sure when Rick left that night, but I fell asleep imagining a hot young Rick Monette with a 1980's asymmetrical skater haircut and a nerdy boyfriend, sitting at the dinner table with Mr. and Mrs. Monette, politely discussing the latest exploits of the literary society.

CHAPTER 23

▼

MAKING THE JUMP

After a few days of being taken care of, I began to resent the whole arrangement. I wasn't angry at Rick, but angry at the situation. I was even like that as a kid with those nasty throat infections. After a while I would get angry, cranky, and ready to go out of the house without my mother "mothering" me. So many of the traits we exhibited as children grew up with us, so that those traits were just hidden in adult issues, even the most basic things like getting cranky when tired or snippy when hungry. I had always felt that men, regardless of sexuality, were the same when it came to our childhood traits strapped on our backs. Rick could get very crabby when things weren't quite going his way, but at all other times he was just happy-go-lucky, a term that he said his second grade teacher used to describe him to his parents. He was just a happy-go-lucky kid who rolled with the punches, and agreed that it was a great thing that this trait came with him into manhood. I got cranky when hungry, tired, or wet, and wrung my hands in worry over the things I couldn't change, and these fantastic abilities continued well into my adulthood.

After Rick left on my fourth day home from the hospital, with at least another eight days to go before the casts would come off, I decided to try taking care of myself. Rick was very understanding, but rightfully doubtful about my ability to do this. After all, he reminded me, I did go to pieces the day before when I had trouble in the shower. That was another issue. As an annoyingly anal clean-freak, the thought of going even one day without bathing made me queasy. The doctor gave me some plastic sheaths and permission to take my arm out of the sling long enough to take a five minute shower, so I had to try this, alone, of course. Rick was there the first time, but I refused to let him see me completely naked yet, much less naked with plaster casts and after nearly a week without "trimming my hedges". My reasoning was that I wasn't going to let him see me hairy and unkempt until we had been together longer and after that one small detail of actually having sex. Even without bathing, seeing Rick every day and watching him do such a manly job of taking care of me made me painfully horny. Madison had insisted that I should take at least two weeks off, with the understanding that she would do everything she could to keep my business going, so there was not even any work to take my mind off of being dirty and horny.

I somehow managed to get my clothes off, lucky that my new boxer shorts had so much give in the waist and such wide leg-holes. I was trying to keep things as normal as possible so I continued sleeping completely in the buff as I had since I left college. The night we kept Stephen on the sofa had been the first time I wore underwear in bed since 1993, even during the winter, so I was not about to let the unfortunate condition of my leg get in the way of my usual life. I stumbled around to brush my teeth and splash some toner on my face, which had the tendency to sweat much more than usual lately with my constant over-exertion. When I look back on that time, I see that I was just being a ridiculous primadonna when the whole thing would have been easier had I just given in, accepted being dirty, greasy hair and all, and accepted Rick's help. But, then again, some things do happen for a reason and the events of that night changed my outlook for good.

I stumped back into my bedroom and got into bed, beginning to feel the effects of the pain medication again. I did discover why people get addicted to painkillers. When I had a couple of those, there was nothing to worry about at all. I think I dozed for a few minutes then woke up again with two of the biggest problems for a semi-ambulatory primadonna, thirst and a full bladder. In my half-drugged yet still compulsively anal state of mind, I decided that I would have to satisfy both before I could even think about going back to sleep. Mustering as much courage as possible, I sat up on the side of the bed, amazed at how I had not fattened up over the past week without any "official" exercise, although the simple act of taking a pee had become much more physical than ever before. As I stood up, my right leg did not seem to want to support me and became really weak, the muscles going into painful cramps.

"Okey-dokey," I thought. "Let's just stand here and exercise it a little. I'm in control here."

I walked one step and hit the floor, luckily pushing my cast out with all of my might before I went down. My freshly polished wood floors caught my bare ass, causing a loud and fairly painful screeching, and there I was, stuck on the floor. It was amusing how I was used to reacting to situations immediately knowing I could count on certain body parts and appendages, so, as I naturally put my arms behind me to hoist myself up on the bed, my right arm, of course, was not available to assist.

Back in high school, when I took Algebra and had ten different kinds of difficulty with it, I infrequently got this flash of pride and success when I finally solved one of the equations that haunted me all through my homework. Sitting there with my ass stuck on the floor nearly twenty years later, the equation was quickly solved: my leverage was at an absolute minimum because the opposing appendages were out of commission.

"God," I sighed. "I may as well not even have opposable thumbs at this point."

I tried to roll over like a beetle on its back but couldn't get far. A couple of times I tried to push myself into a standing position with my right leg but it just didn't work. I was able to scoot myself across the floor in a broken crab walk, but the floor did not allow my skin to glide smoothly and there was only so much raising and lowering I could do. The doctor had given me some exercises to do while I was confined at home, but I put those aside because I viewed myself as healthier and more in shape than most thirty-five year old men.

"Dammit!" I yelled, and swung my left arm like a punch, which brought me again to the floor. I was sweating profusely by this time and was increasingly groggy from the pain medication, and to top it off, I was now totally angry at the world. I lay there for a while, just staring at the ceiling.

Since I knew I wasn't getting anywhere and needed badly to empty my pea-sized bladder, I decided to call Rick. Luckily I had stuffed my cell phone in my iPod sport strap and velcroed it to my left arm, where it stayed. Before dialing, I again thought about my total dependence at that moment, and egged on by the drugs, burst into tears. When I thought about being a naked thirty-five year old in a cast with my butt glued to the wood floor, I cried harder. I cried for being angry, for being stressed, and for losing my independence, even temporarily. I cried because my caged up teary emotion was just hanging out there in my mind, poisoning me and making it hard for me to move forward. After a few minutes of this, I gathered my composure so as not to continually break my mother's rule, and called Rick.

"Chello?" he said, sleepily.

"I'm stuck," I whined again.

"Be right over," he replied with a tone of voice that said "I told you so".

While I lay there waiting on him, resigned to the fact that Rick was about to see me naked anyway, I thought about everything again. It was time for me to move on, to stop feeling sorry for myself about losing Ayers and now about being temporarily out of service. It was time for me to stop feeling guilty about having a relationship with Stephen that was just about the sex. After all, he was a willing party to this as well. It was time for me to let out my feelings, which were a mix of anger and regret. I was angry at Rick for making me fall for him and having to choose between dealing with his HIV and not having him at all. I was regretful because I had taken so long to make a decision, like I was buying a house or a car, when human emotions were at play.

"Oh my God!" Rick shouted. "Baby, what happened to you?"

I had not heard him come in, so he startled me enough to make me jump. Then the tears came again.

"I have to piss," I wailed, and then simply had a primadonna collapse.

Rick did not seem fazed by the whole naked thing, so I literally just let it all hang out. He leaned over me for a second and then hoisted me up onto the bed.

"Are you hurt?" he asked, wiping my tears with his thumbs.

I shook my head. Rick pulled me to him, my head coming to rest on his stomach, his hands softly caressing my back. Then he started laughing.

"Why …" he could not complete his question because of his laughter. "Why didn't you just call me? You're so damned stubborn. I told you I'm happy to help you out. Geez. Your ass was stuck to the floor."

With that, he laughed harder and then helped me into the bathroom. As I stood over the toilet, he stayed behind me and I let him. He helped me back to bed and brought me a glass of water with a warning not to drink much of it or we would have to go back through all of this again.

"Even with the cast and all," he said, his eyes cast downward, "you're still hot."

"Goddamit!" I yelled. "I am so mad at you for making me fall for you! This is the hardest decision I have yet to make in my life and I am just so fucking mad about it!"

My voice had taken on a tone that Rick had not yet had the pleasure of hearing, so he just stood there, gawking slightly at this little naked madman in front of him.

"You waltz into my life and complicate things," I ranted, "and then I fall in love with you …"

There it was, my truest inner feeling just gushing out of me, something I was not used to. My body always had a strange way of dealing with things, from too much dairy to too much unaired emotion. In this case, my body waited until I was naked and stuck to a floor with a full bladder to blab.

"And I have to face the fact that I am so goddamned afraid of losing you that I haven't been able to see what fun it would be to really be together," my voice quivered and I took a ragged gasp. "And now I've made you go through all of this caretaking for me when I haven't even asked you anymore about your feelings since you told me you had fallen in love with me …"

He came over and sat on the bed with me, watching my tears fall silently again, and put his arm around me.

"Hey, hey." he said quietly to calm me down, "Hey."

He turned my face toward his. "It's okay to be mad," he said. "I understand that. We really have no choice about who comes in and out of our lives. And it's okay that you haven't asked me about my feelings. I told you how I felt and expected that to be part of your, um, decision-making process."

I made an attempt to smile while Rick leaned in closer. We kissed, at first lightly, and then the kiss turned into a passionate yet clumsy embrace. When I pulled back, I remembered that I was buck naked, and on pain pills, my state of being turned on was quite obvious. Rick spied this and had to make a comment.

"Well, well, mister," he said, smiling. "I see that it still works. This is really great, you know, better than Manlink. I'm getting a live preview and not just a five year old photo."

I sat there for a moment, wondering if he was going to go ahead and take advantage of the situation. The algebraic equations came back, in the form of solving the problem of how we would even manage to make love in my condition.

"I'm afraid I have the wrong kind of sling," I laughed.

"We are definitely not doing this now," Rick informed me. "I'm gonna wait on you. I know how you feel and I know that we have some catching up to do. Now put that away."

The last statement came with a nod toward my deflating member, which I pulled the sheet over. Rick massaged my leg, working the cramps out, while I stared in wonder at him. Even after an outburst, complete with tears and cursing, he was trying to make me feel better.

"So, how did you come out?" he asked.

"It wasn't much of a stretch," I replied.

Like Rick, my high school years had been spent in the company of the other "misfits" and with "girl friends" but no girlfriend. I think the excuse I used was that I needed to concentrate on getting educated, although I still managed to have a social life. In college, I joined a fraternity simply to throw people off of my trail, to distract everyone I knew from assuming that I was gay. The frat boy life offered an array of manly pursuits, including sorority girls, but that part of the life passed me by. I did my share of drinking and smoking, and even became an officer in the fraternity to be able to keep some things in my control. After a few years with no girlfriends, especially through college, my parents sat me down and flat out asked me if I had "anyone special". At the time I didn't, so I told them no, thinking it would be the end of the conversation.

"We want you to be happy," my father had said, as spokesman for the couple, "and we are okay if there is something else you want to tell us."

My mother smiled encouragingly as my father looked at me, his eyes denoting the trust that we had had for so many years.

"Since you put it that way," I had stated bluntly, "I am gay. I don't have a boyfriend, so if you know anybody be sure to hook me up."

This explanation was so similar to the one Rick had given me a few nights before that we might as well have told the same story. Rick kicked off his sandals and lay down in the bed next to me, mercifully leaving his clothes on.

"Can I talk to Madison and Stuart about this whole thing?" I asked, hoping this question would not be too forward.

"Well, I guess," Rick answered, "but there are very few people who know that I'm positive. Just tell them to keep it under their hats, you know?"

"And your parents?" I mumbled.

"Not yet," he replied softly. "Not yet."

The last thing I remember was Rick rolling over to put his arm across me. This time it was different; his arm had a feeling of permanence, like it had been doing the same thing for years. I was ready to call us what we were, a couple, and realized the split second before I fell back to sleep that we had made the jump from "just friends" to "together" some time ago.

CHAPTER 24

▼

A TRIO OF CONFESSIONS

My boredom reached a fever pitch a couple of days before my doctor visit. Rick was a fixture in the bed next to me every night but had returned to work, promising that he could be back in five minutes if I needed him. I had been doing the ridiculous-looking exercises the doctor prescribed, so my legs were feeling better and the good one could hold me up again, even on repeated visits to the toilet. To break the boredom, I begged Madison and Stuart to grab lunch and bring it to my apartment, a task they both balked at but carried out because of their sarcastic devotion. I moved quickly to the door when they arrived, and Stuart nearly knocked me down parading through the door in mock hysteria.

"Girl!" he shouted. "Can you drink yet? 'Cause I took the rest of the day away from the clients. I'm gonna go home and take a nap so I can go out boy-huntin' tonight!"

I rolled my eyes and helped Madison with a file I'd asked her to bring. She had reminded me repeatedly to have my remote access set up to the firm's network but I never did.

"See why I've told you over and over again to get your virtual network access?" she asked impatiently with her usual smile.

"Sorry," I said, and then changed my tune. "Hey, you guys need to be nice to me. I'm traumatized, dammit."

Stuart, who had already begun to put out the food like a good Southern host, began a story in his loudest voice. "Ya'll don't know from traumatized!" he shouted, twisting his neck around a few times. "Remember that guy I was doing named Mark? The twenty-year-old with all of the tattoos? Well, honeys, I was cruising the park last night and there he was, trying to turn some tricks. Now, I'm traumatized!"

Madison and I looked at each other knowingly. Stuart had told the exact same story a couple of years before, except the guy's name was Paulie or something just as disturbing, and he was on the top end of Stuart's age range, at about twenty-five. Stuart's tendency toward the younger guys also made him the target of hot young hustlers, who could use a man until he just got turned off. Paulie even got a Gucci jacket out of the deal, which Stuart referred to as the cost of beauty or some such thing. Privately, Madison and I always debated the source of Stuart's nonchalant attitude toward sex, commitment, and men of the same age. He was brought into a strict Southern Baptist family who went to church at every opportunity and believed that hell was going to be full of Catholics and homosexuals. After Southern Baptist college, Stuart "converted" to Catholicism simply for the shock value, going to family Christmas dinner and insisting on saying a couple of rosaries over the turkey. After his father regained his holier-than-thou composure, he asked Stuart to keep his idolatry to himself. He got a good chuckle out of it and the next year, again at Christmas, Stuart talked one of his female friends into coming to the dinner with him to announce that they were together. This particular female friend happened to be a black lesbian with no current love interest, so she gladly went along to "flip the white Baptists out." In between Christmases, Stuart was happily screwing younger guys who would dump him when they found out he didn't have money. He wasn't happy with that situation, so I always made the guess that his need to be needed made him happy to blow money, which he now had plenty of, on his young men.

After the "lesbian Christmas" Stuart refused to officially come out to his parents but, at every opportunity, came up with ways to further irritate them. At one Easter gathering, which was supposed to be followed by a church service, Stuart had gotten a few henna tattoos and a few magnetic earrings to make a dramatic effect. Finally, after at least five or six years of jokes, he wrote a letter to his mother and dad, and very seriously explained that his sexuality was no joke and that he would appreciate it if they could just deal with it.

"After all," he explained to me one night after a few cocktails, "my mother always complemented me on my fucking drapes. Did I have to draw a picture?"

So at our impromptu lunch that day, Madison and I were not shocked to hear that one of Stuart's boys had gone hooker.

"Anyway," he continued, coming over to me, "how's my little crippled buddy?"

"Fine."

"And how's your new stud?"

"Grrrr."

"Finally," sighed Madison.

"How did you do it with all of your casts and stuff?" Stuart asked, forever looking for the intimate details.

"You've both got the wrong end of the stick," I explained, "because we haven't, um, been, ah, intimate yet."

The two of them just stared at me, a scene from a stage comedy.

"I know," I said, exasperated. "If I don't hurry he'll be off to some other pasture or farm or whatever it is you say."

"I'm just amazed you've held out this long," said Madison. "You've been a walking orgasm since I've known you."

I debated about the entire explanation, but then decided to go ahead. I have always been unable to come to grips with anything, especially an issue as large as moving on with Rick, without bouncing it off of someone, typically Madison or Stuart. Despite our professional and friendly relationships, they were both sensible people who could always shed light on some weird situation. They stayed by my side during Ayers' illness, and were the first people who came after he died. That day I sat in the hospital room with him in a state of complete numbness, watching him for any sign of life although he had already gone. He looked so peaceful, like he was sleeping, with no pain and no other emotion except bliss on his face. I herded his family out so that I could be there alone, and I stayed for an hour until Madison and Stuart arrived. When they came in the room Madison came over and sat down next to me, with her hand on my shoulder, silently. Stuart stood over the bed quietly looking from me back to his friend Ayers repeatedly.

After what seemed like hours, Madison spoke. "Honey," she said. "Let's talk about what we're going to do now."

From there, she took charge of calling the funeral home, arranging to have him taken away, and getting me home. Stuart, although very useful for quiet moral support, was not the know-it-all rock he usually was.

Now that I was facing another challenge, I knew that they could help me make sense of it. As we were eating our lunch-sized pastas and sipping sparkling water, I made the move to start talking.

"Um," I said, then cleared my throat.

"Empty your mouth before talking, you pig," admonished Stuart. "I know you weren't raised in no barn, Doreen."

I glared at him for a moment and continued, "As I was saying, uh-hmm, I have to get something off of my chest."

"Wait!" Madison interrupted. "We haven't had anything to drink yet!"

"Meet Betty Ford;" I said to Stuart.

"Shuh-huh," Stuart replied.

"Okay," I finally had the nerve to spill it. "There is one tiny issue with Rick. I think I can deal with it, but I have to talk about it before it drives me nuts."

"Don't *tell* me he's a power-bottom," interjected Stuart.

"Can you get your mind out of your pants for just one *second*?" I shot back.

"Please," Madison added. "He's a man and when you're a man that's all you think about. How do you think I ended up with two kids? With a man who really thinks with the brain in the head on top of his shoulders? I don't think so."

"Look," I said, the tone of urgency coming out easily. "Can you just let me finish? I've totally fallen for him. I could see this. I could see us together. So here's the problem. He has HIV."

I paused for what I thought would be a dramatic reaction, but there was none.

"Okay," Stuart piped up first, already an expert in the AIDS/HIV area, having been tested once in a lifetime of backseat hopping. "That *is* an issue, but certainly something we can work with in this day and age. What's the problem? Are you scared of getting it or scared that he could die on you?"

"Well," I said, firmly realizing one truth for the first time, "I'm not afraid of getting it, I guess. Safe sex is the norm, and … well, the other sex issues have a very small incidence of transmission. Those are risks I'm willing to take. I mean, I think about Stephen and wonder where *that* had been before I got hold of it … even *while* I was getting hold of it."

"You have a point there, although a disgusting one," Madison said, putting her hand on my arm. "But it sounds like you are afraid of losing him."

I nodded and Madison went into a story that I never thought I would hear from her. A year earlier, Madison explained, she had gone to a charity function and met an old friend and his wife. This old friend, apparently not quite old and still a total hottie, took her onto the dance floor and by doing this took her out of her usual routine. They met for lunch a few days later and then at the French Quarter Inn one night later. They made love like neither of them ever had, with so much trapped boredom with their current situations that it seemed like the natural thing to do. For Madison the next day was hell, feeling painfully guilty as she watched her children and her husband going about their daily lives as if nothing had happened. Her hot friend, though, took the sex as a sign that he and Madison were meant to be together, and as a token of that feeling sent an expensive pearl necklace to her office. She tried to return the pearls to him, telling him that he should give them to his wife and forget that the whole thing happened. He insisted that she keep the pearls as a reminder that she was in the wrong relationship if she had let this happen between the two of them.

She did not see her friend again, even though she ran into his wife every once in a while at Lord & Taylor and guiltily explained that she was late to pick up the kids. Madison held on to the pearls, never wearing them until the day she walked into Pepe's Pawn to get rid of her scarlet letter, and with several thousand in her pocket, returned home to confess to Peter what she had done. Peter was angry for two weeks, even creeping into the guest bedroom after the kids had gone to sleep, with no desire to even look at his wife. Finally, he forgave her, with the warning that another action like that would cause him to leave, take the kids, and make sure that she never saw them again. They took a vacation using the money from the pearls and did not look back.

"The point here," Madison said, as Stuart and I stared with bugged out eyes and absolutely no movement whatsoever, "is that I was afraid I had lost Peter. I prepared myself for him to walk out, take the kids, and leave me alone with that big house to knock around in. When I knew I wasn't going to lose him, the world turned bright again. You've already lost someone, so you know what that's like. If you're prepared, every day that he's with you will be bright. Think about it. It's simple and icky-sweet, but true. Besides, as you so nicely demonstrated, it only takes some freak in a minivan to whack you, anyway."

Madison and I turned to Stuart, hoping for a reply from his point of view.

"HIV or no," he said blankly, "be thankful you've found someone. Even if it's short, which I really hope it's not because I don't want to deal with another dramatic funereal situation here, be glad he's there for you. Be goddamned glad he can be there for you. I fall for losers because I'm afraid to find a real commitment ..."

The third confession came so quickly that we didn't have time to react.

"Should we go in the closet for confession?" I asked him with a smile.

"Mark," he said wistfully, swirling angel hair absent-mindedly with his fork. "Mark I think I loved. For some reason, he just made me feel young and fun and sexy, when really I'm only one out of three. Obviously Rick has it for you, and you have it for him. What could be better? By the way, if you two make a porn video I'll pay good money to see it."

I started feeling relieved almost immediately after unburdening myself, and as usual, saw that a discussion of a problem was much better than keeping it inside. I thought about how many times I had stayed mad at Ayers for something which now seemed trivial, knowing that just getting it out in the open would have made everyone feel better right away. This open conversation that had just occurred between my two friends and me also glaringly reminded me that everyone had their issues, each issue serious because it was unique to that person. I tried to imagine what a relationship could be like if it was completely out in the open and realized that this was the relationship I had with Rick.

"Thank you both," I said, looking Madison and Stuart in the eyes. "I feel so much better just having talked about it."

"What are friends for, Doreen?" Stuart asked.

"If either of you queens says a thing about the pearl necklace," Madison warned us. "I will *kill* you both."

"I understand," I said. "The same goes for my story. Rick doesn't let people know and he won't until it becomes absolutely necessary."

"Oh please," said Stuart. "I should go ahead and kill you both since you know I'm human."

"Somehow," I said, "I think I've known that all along, Feathers."

Our lunch ended with a group hug, our friendships stronger through the power of confession and with my thoughts about Rick neatly sorted out.

CHAPTER 25

▼

IT'S MORE THAN SEX NOW

The following Friday, Rick took me to the doctor to get the casts off, a process which freaked me out more than the accident and all of the uncomfortable moments afterwards. He held my hand through the whole experience, in which the doctor used a little saw to open the plaster and to give me a near breakdown. I was given a soft brace, which was supposed to be worn during waking hours and over my clothing, for my leg, another prospect that made me freak. After all, I had been wearing boxer shorts for two weeks while trapped in the house. I needed to put on a pair of ass-lifting Earl Jeans and go somewhere other than my livingroom. But, the time spent in captivity was not that bad when Rick was around. He made a point of coming over every day after his afternoon workout and staying all night. Seeing him comfortable in my bed, briefs and all, had made me want him even more than ever. I was in love with him and ready to deal with any of the things that could come our way. We had already dealt with something major and Rick was now accustomed to the diva-like fits and ultra crankiness that came with my temporary disability. When I walked out of the doctor's office, with him walking close to steady me, I felt like I was finally in control of the whole situation.

He drove me immediately to the BMW dealership, where I selected a bright red sedan with tan leather and a sunroof and leased it on the spot. I was finished with convertibles and trying to find a way to identify myself with the perceived sexiness of my car. The junior executive model was fine with me, and Rick told me how sexy I looked in it, much to the half-hearted amusement of the salesman. After the deal was closed, Rick went home when I promised to keep my phone handy and call him if I needed any help. We agreed to meet later so that I could drop by the rehabilitation center to visit Stephen, something that the accident and its aftermath had seriously postponed. I noted then that Rick was completely at ease with time alone, time that was to be devoted to the care of his own mind and body and not mine, another good sign. I called Stephen and told him to go to the window to see the car in an attempt to keep his mind off being in a rehab center, even for a few minutes. He looked older sober and seemed to have a calmness that he didn't have before.

"Dude!" He greeted me with a hug. "That's a hot car. You look good in it. Change is good."

"Right on, Dude," I smiled as Stephen took me to the large visiting area of the center.

The visitor's area was more like a big hotel lobby with tables, chairs, and over-stuffed Pottery Barn knockoff sofas, a comfortable place for confronting your addict. We stood and faced each other for a second, and then Stephen reached over to hug me again. He suggested that we take a walk outside on the grounds, even though it was overly humid.

As we walked, Stephen tried to put his words together. "I wanted to apologize," he said slowly, "for causing you so many problems. I'm sorry."

"You weren't that much trouble," I replied with a wink.

"Too much trouble for you," he answered back with his usual sharpness. "By the way, you didn't help the situation any by decking Nick. I didn't want to say anything while you were recovering."

I realized that the topic of Nick had not come up in any of the quick phone calls Stephen made while I was at home with the casts. I didn't know if it was his newfound maturity or my own selfishness that had caused this.

"I feel really bad," I said, "and I would really like to apologize to him for the whole thing. I'm a lover not a fighter, Dude."

Stephen continued, not needing to tell me where the situation stood between him and Nick.

"No need to apologize to him. Nick was okay. Well, he was pissed until you had your accident and then he was okay. He said it was, like, karma, you know. You decked him and then some dude in a minivan decked you."

"He said that, did he?" I asked, angry for a second. Then, the protective nature came back.

"Listen," I looked him straight in the eye. "I'm just going to say this once, and then I'm going to leave it alone, as much as a big-mouthed Italian can leave something alone. You need to be careful. I don't think this thing with Nick is right for you. Just be careful."

I thought Stephen was going to argue, something he did well, but we had not noticed the huge storm cloud that was blowing up behind us, and we were not within running distance when the rain started to fall. We looked around for a place to go and hurried into a gazebo a short distance from where we were standing when the first thunderclap let loose. Our serious conversation turned into the comedy of two screaming queens trying to get out of a thunderstorm before we could continue it. My leg, in the brace, was really throbbing from the quick walk to the gazebo. We sat inside it, sheltered by a thick bunch of trees, for a few seconds before Stephen reacted calmly to my warning that the relationship with Nick was not right.

"I get it, Alex," he finally said. "Thanks for sticking with me. I have to make my own decisions, you know? It's something I haven't done in a long time. Just tell me that you like, support me and all."

"I do, like, support you," I answered. "I just want you to be careful. We've come too far to get you screwed up again."

Stephen stared at me for a second as the thunder rumbled again, and then moved closer. I was startled, hoping that he was just going to tell me something secretive, but he leaned forward and made an attempt to kiss me, which I backed out of. He grabbed my arm and pulled himself up on it when I braced my injured leg. Stephen stood there, looking at me while I struggled for the power to back away and say something. He put his arm around my waist and pulled again.

"You know I can't resist you," he said earnestly. "It's been a while since I had sex."

I rolled my eyes heavily, while I found the right words.

"Have you lost your damned mind?" I asked. "Why in the hell do you think I'm interested in sex with you?"

"I thought …" he said, and then stopped.

"Stephen," I said. "You're really confused. That's why you just need to take it easy. No sex. No dates. Nothing. I'm with Rick now. Besides, I don't feel that way for you anymore. What I'm trying to say is that I feel friendship for you, but this is not a 'fringe benefit' sort of friendship. We're friends and that's all. We are not friends who screw."

Stephen looked a little disappointed, and I wondered if he already knew the state of our friendship but wanted to try for a little rainy afternoon canoodle anyway.

"Sorry," he said, not quite convincingly. "I knew we were friends but I thought maybe you'd still like to have sex every once in a while. Sorry."

The rain stopped just at the right time, and as we walked back to the building, I began to feel better about Stephen's pass at me, noting that his confusion was probably at a high point and not to hold it against him. He apologized a couple more times before we ever made it back to the fake Pottery Barn room, but I repeated that it was all right.

He hugged me tight before I left, warning me to take it easy on my damaged parts. Now that Rick was all I saw, being close to Stephen was like hugging my brother, and the mishap of a pass that he made at me in the gazebo set that feeling into stone. One of my inherited traits was the ability to stick my nose in where it didn't belong and keep it there, so it was difficult for me to let go and let Stephen make a right or wrong decision, especially since he had taken the right place in my life. When I got to the car, I took the brace off, threw it in the back seat, and walked around the parking lot a couple of times. I was finally feeling like myself, which meant that I could go home, take a shower, and even get dressed without help.

As I drove, I thought about how I could not take my own physical freedom for granted ever again. I had much more empathy for people who could not take care of themselves and vowed to myself that I would maintain that empathy, even if I ended up taking care of Rick someday. Then I got angry for thinking that way, vowing again to assume daily that Rick was going to be independent for the rest of his life.

The shower was like a dip in the pool on the hottest day of summer, a refreshing cleansing that made me feel even better. I was off the pain medication and felt whole for the first time in weeks. I also felt major physical needs rising up, along with constant butterflies in the pit of my stomach as I thought about Rick and how I wanted to be with him. The dilemma became whether or not I should plan our first time together or just let it happen, my mind playing all kinds of possible scenarios while I moisturized, stretched, and rolled around in my freshly washed sheets. Rick was now in my every thought, everything I could possibly think of somehow came back to him, my relationship with him, my feelings for him and his feelings for me. Everything in me was waking up, all of me feeling things I hadn't felt since the night I met Ayers and since every day with him. I knew it was time to let go of the past, let go of the commitment I still held to Ayers, knowing that moving on with someone else was not a breach of that commitment. I could hear his voice in my head, telling me it was okay to keep going, to be in love again, and to be in love with someone that could be taken away.

I sat up abruptly in the bed and mechanically got up to find some clothes, slipping into a pair of jeans, my sandals, and a sleeveless t-shirt, not an impressive ensemble but something that would cover me up long enough to get to Rick. I left my apartment with one thing on my mind.

When Rick answered the door, he was in his camouflage shorts again, along with a white t-shirt, looking startled that I was there.

"Alex?" he asked through big eyes. "Are you okay?"

"I'm fine," I answered, "and I love you."

"Guess what?" he asked playfully. "I love you, too."

With that, he grabbed me, pulling me to him so that my head came to rest on his chest, his hands caressing my back with a strong grip. We kissed, not the kisses of the past few weeks, but a kiss that involved tongues, teeth, lips, and some razor burn from five o'clock shadow. I could not release my liplock on him until I helped him pull his t-shirt over his head, revealing that tan, muscular body that I had wanted to be this close to again and for real. As my lips began to move across his chest, his skin smelling of vanilla bodywash, soft to the touch yet still a man's skin, I tightened my grip around his back. We looked at each other, sure that this was the right time, and tightly holding on to each other, went to his bedroom.

As our clothes came off, I was ready to shout that I was going to make love to the man I had fallen for. His body, now mine to explore, was tight, hard, and muscular, but of a softness that invited me to run my hands over every curve, every muscle, and every pore. I could not get enough of his skin on my lips, his taste something that was unique to him but almost familiar to me. I could not feel enough of him, grasping him and trying to pull him even closer than he was.

The evening light coming in through the bedroom window made a contrasting pattern on our bodies as we slowly began to explore each other, finding the parts that made us laugh, or shiver, or gasp. This was my ultimate fantasy, the fantasy that I had not quite identified but knew existed somewhere in my mind, the fantasy of again making love to someone that I could not get enough of. There were moments that night when we stopped everything to sit up, face each other on our knees in the bed, and drink in our nakedness, the final shedding of any of the constraints we had before. I watched him quiver as I ran my fingers down his stomach, tracing the indention of each muscle, following the downward slope of the "v" of his torso. He felt me tense and gasp as he kissed my neck then kissed his way down to my chest, and then watched me laugh as he lightly tickled my stomach with his tongue. I found out that my lips on his inner thighs caused him to groan with pleasure and laugh at the same time, a five star erotic experience.

After what turned out to be hours of pure carnality, standing nude in the doorway of the bedroom, illuminated by the streetlights, Rick was beautiful, the Adonis that I thought he was the first time he had invited me there. I can't remember how many times we made love that night, each time becoming more emotional yet more physical, more intimate yet more uninhibited. For two men nearing forty, our sex drives were raging, our need for each other greater than we had felt at any point in our relationship before.

At about three in the morning, we found some cheese and crackers and a bottle of red wine and shared it from a tray in the middle of the bed, not finding it necessary to get dressed or even sit up. I sat on top of him as he lounged back on a pile of pillows, his hands behind his head, his biceps pumped, as we talked about the trivial things that come up in every day conversation. A bag of M&M's made it into the bed around five, partially for fun and partially for desert, Rick lining up the green ones starting at my belly button, because green M&M's were the horny ones.

As the daylight started coming through the window, we were in the middle of making love again, this time sweating, groaning, and whispering over and over how in love we were. That night, our relationship changed, from a "could be" to an "is", from immaturity to maturity, to something that was now real and tangible, the thing that we thought would be a problem now neatly discussed and packed away.

We dozed for a few hours, and when I woke up, I found myself nestled on a pillow that was resting between Rick's body and his arm, the most comfortable place I had been since Ayers' death. It had happened, and it happened when I was the least concerned and the least worried about the future, and more concerned about living the here and now. I had moved on.

CHAPTER 26

▼

TAKE YOUR TURN

"Gawd!" drawled Madison in her mocking Southern belle voice as I walked back into the office for the first time in two weeks. "Someone has a glow that did not come from recovering at home for two weeks!"

She hugged me and walked with me toward my office, where everyone else was waiting with a "Welcome Back" banner, bagels, and coffee. It was touching, but I couldn't wait to get home and hang out with Rick, which was the only thing on my mind. Jen gave me a hug and a wink, that knowing wink that Madison must have taught her just that very morning.

As I faced my work once again, I thought about how my work required calculated risk, just like my life required calculated risk. I finally felt good about both work and personal, knowing that my abilities had been tested and proven. I was back in the swing within a few hours and even more anxious to get home after a few dirty phone calls from Rick, who explained in graphic detail what he was going to do with me as soon as we were back in bed together. Our entire weekend had been spent in bed, venturing out only for food and the gym but otherwise staying close and having awesome sex.

My mind, which always had the tendency to be a scary place, had already catalogued and compared the sexual stuff. Ayers and I had a very strong emotional connection but a fairly immature sex life, something that I didn't know then, because the sex was the best I had known at the time. With Stephen, the sexual draw was his youth; that young, smooth body, the knowledge that the guy choosing to be in my bed was thirteen years my junior, the feeling of control that I got from having a relationship with him. Until that point, the meaningless one night stands or month long relationships left me feeling out of control, so Stephen helped me trade emotional attachment for that control. Having sex with Stephen was pretty steamy, though, and many of those encounters stayed vividly in my memory.

With Rick, it was the first mature relationship of my entire life, both emotionally and physically, an admission that made me wonder where the years went. The physical relationship with Rick was an extension of the emotional one, every touch, every sigh, every groan, moan, or grunt a sign of our true feelings for each other. Never before had I been able to say "I love you" back to someone during sex, never before had I been able to let my guard down at all. For once, I didn't suck my stomach in to make it look more muscular when I was with Rick, or position myself just perfectly beneath the sheet to look as enticing as possible, because Rick simply did not care. I looked the same on the outside, but my inside was so refreshed that it was hard to contain.

That afternoon, I went to the gym right after work and found no need to look around because I just wasn't interested. The picture in my mind was of Rick, stretched out naked on the bed, his hands behind his head, his biceps pumped up, that beautiful tan skin giving off just enough of a glow to be luminous, the line of a one-inch bathing suit showing off a contrast that drew my eyes right to the middle, his sexy legs still muscled even though they were at rest, his nicely manicured toes putting the final touch on the body. Even more than that, the picture of him in this position was smiling at me, his green eyes flashing and that perfect hair finally messed completely up from the friction of sleep, sex, and the constant presence of my hands running through it. How amazing that I was suddenly mature because the right someone appeared in my life.

When I got home, Rick came over immediately, and without a word, grabbed me and kissed me, hard and deep. As he started to paw me, I weakly protested that I was just back from the gym, that I was sweaty and dirty.

"Mmmmm," he growled in my ear. "Dirty is okay, too, but why don't we clean up?"

We ended up doing the actual cleaning in the shower in cold water because the hot water just didn't last long enough, running out right after our second time, Rick's breath over my shoulder fogging up the shaving mirror. We didn't cook that night, either because we were just too into each other to worry about it. Mandy's Deli had been to our building so many times in the past three weeks that they knew us and rushed our food because we were such good tippers.

The night Mandy herself delivered, she pegged it. "Newlyweds, right?" she had asked, her cigarette-stained voice taking on a note of sarcasm. Rick and I laughed really hard over that one.

I had just smeared chocolate icing from a cupcake on Rick's nipples when his cell rang. The interruption was enough to bother us, but we didn't budge, so I went on licking the icing until a knock on my door brought it all to a halt. As I got up, I tried to lick any final traces of the icing off of him but had trouble seeing in the dim light of my living room. I turned the music down and went to the back door, shocked out of my head to see Nick standing there, looking sober and fairly harmless.

"Um, honey?" I shouted back to Rick. "Can you come here please?"

Rick padded into the kitchen, still in his boxers, with chocolate icing on his chest and now on his right arm.

"What is it?" he asked as I opened the door with Nick on the other side.

"Oh," he acted suitably disappointed, and then turned back to me as Nick spoke.

"Sorry guys," he said. "I just needed to tell you that I'm leaving. Um, you've got some chocolate or something on your arm there."

Rick and I looked at each other and reluctantly let Nick in. We offered him a seat in the livingroom, which he took, uncomfortably. I decided to try to save the day, knowing well that any of us who had living exes usually had them in our lives in some way or another. Stephen was a great example of that, an ex-boyfriend who hung around. Gay guys did this automatically, I always felt, because the intimacy achieved with a lover could carry over into everyday confidences. Many gay guys could have close relationships with family but chose to have close relationships with men they had already seen naked.

"Look, Nick," I said. "I'm really sorry for hitting you that night. I got a little stressed."

"It's okay," he replied. "No damage done. Anyway, I'm sorry to show up like this. I wonder how Rick would react if your ex showed up without warning."

"Well," I said, "one's in rehab and the other is technically dead, so if he showed up we would probably have a hell of a lot more to worry about."

I smiled my best beauty contestant smile, to which neither Rick nor Nick responded.

"So," Rick said impatiently, "you're going back to Atlanta?"

"Yeah," he said slowly. "Things just didn't work out the way I wanted them to."

"How's that?" I asked, wondering what new turn had occurred with Stephen.

"Well," Nick said, "Stephen isn't thrilled about going to Atlanta. He's not coming with, so I guess that pretty much means it's over."

I was relieved to hear that Stephen had made this choice, the choice to get himself together before he entered yet another relationship, much less move away from everything he had known for so long. I was secretly hoping that some sense had rubbed off on him, then stopped myself from having this thought. Just like my mother I assumed that anyone who was not thinking like me was not thinking in the most sensible way. Maybe Stephen was just an impulsive person who enjoyed being impulsive. I had never been able to make a move without chewing it over, dissecting it, discussing it, until I was sick of it. Not only was fear a factor in my life, I was also a person who could be driven by fear of the unknown, like when I turned down the lead in the school play in first grade. The class performed a children's version of the Kipling story about the elephant and his trunk and my teacher thought I would be great as the narrator, the most visible role in the whole play. I turned it down, afraid of what people would think if I messed up; the role went to Ashley Kean who became one of the most popular kids in high school, a cheerleader dating the captain of the football team. My grandparents talked about this incident until I was well into my twenties, when for the last time, they pointed out how popular Ashley had becoome. I emphatically announced that I wished it had been me who took that role as the narrator so that I could have married the captain of the high school football team, stayed home, and raised kids.

Nick had continued speaking while I was regressing to 1977, so I decided to tune back in.

"… I mean it," he was saying, "I messed up."

Rick had this strange look on his face.

"I'm sorry," I said. "What?"

Nick spoke flatly. "I just told Rick he should just come back with me instead of starting over."

I turned to Rick, my shock plainly evident on my face. Nick went on.

"Come on Rick, this guy decked me," he said, jerking his hand in my direction. "So you think he's not violent either? I was willing to deal with the HIV thing and you just cut me off. I made you into what you are … you were a skinny twink with bleached hair when I plucked you off the Stairmaster …"

I raised my eyebrows, inviting Rick to explain. "They were lowlights," he said indignantly. "They were reddish lowlights, not bleached like pretty boy here."

Rick narrated a brief story to fill me in while Nick stood impatiently to one side. They met at the gym, Rick happily plugging away on the stair climber day by day, keeping neither fat nor muscle on his body, really a tall, good looking yet very skinny six footer. Nick showed him how to work out, how to balance it all in order to keep some muscle and look great. Rick viewed it as Nick's need to control someone and also took the chance to deny the fact that he was a twink. I really didn't care about this stroll down Strange Memory Lane because I was more concerned about the fact that this guy had marched into my house and asked my boyfriend to go with him back to Atlanta.

I had lived out my ultimate fantasy with Rick over and over again in the past week, having sex for hours while he told me he loved me right in my ear. Now I was facing the ultimate nightmare, the secret inferiority that I had always held now boiling to the top. What if this was simply a break for Rick, one of those things that was good while it lasted but not for real? My fear of the unknown was not uncommon, but not something I had seen in Rick. What if this was one of his deep fears, this unknown? It would be easy to go back to a comfortable place, especially if you were suddenly put in the position of being the one with the advantage. Then I thought about Nick, his violent, passive-aggressive nature that made him need to pick on someone, the fact that he had physically attacked Rick more than once. Could Rick possibly be that afraid? Add in the fact that Rick had something that could make him sick and even kill him, the fact that he might have to rely on someone to take care of him. That alone could make him want to take advantage of the offer of a familiar space, a familiar face, and the promise that all would be nice again.

I was scared suddenly, scared that I was going to watch this whole thing fall apart right in front of my eyes, that this guy that I viewed as my knight in shining armor was going to walk out. I could not see that this was an irrational fear, especially knowing about what really went on between them, but my mind always reacted that way. Some time in the 90's, a geologist predicted that the New Madrid fault would create a huge earthquake that was going to knock Memphis, St. Louis, Vicksburg, and New Orleans into the river, even down to the day. We all knew this was a ridiculous prediction, but nonetheless that day my fear kept me from driving the usual route to my college classes because there were too many bridges. Irrational fear always seemed to take over and paralyze me even when the back of my mind was completely rational. I sat down on the sofa, staring straight ahead, not able to say anything.

"Are you kidding?" Rick asked. "You have *got* to be joking. You were just a stop along the road, Nick. You treated me like shit."

Then Rick became angry, something I had not yet seen, his voice rising to a garbled shout, the tears welling in his eyes.

"You hit me!" he shouted at Nick. "You pushed me. You gave me a fucking black eye. I had to explain to everyone that I got into a bar fight. Even the straightest of the straight know that the gays don't have bar fights! For Christ's sake, Nick, you may have goddamned well killed me a couple of times … and you get this look in your eyes that's just not you, it's this mad look that made me think that you were fucking possessed! Forget about AIDS, Jesus, I go with you and I don't have to worry about that because one step out of line and you'll take care of nature for me, won't you? Won't you, you fucking moronic bully, you asshole!"

Rick had picked up a candlestick from the coffee table, actually a cheap candlestick that may not have put a dent in Nick's head like he wanted it to, and was standing there, breathing hard, almost sobbing, a few tears running down his cheeks, holding it like he was going to swing it. I took his hand and lowered the candlestick, then looked at him.

"Do you have anything else to say?" I asked softly, holding his wrist tightly just in case he wanted to deck Nick just like I did.

"Yes," he said, looking at Nick. "I forgive you."

I gave Nick one of my dirtiest looks, like the one I gave him before I decked him the night of my accident, and he walked. Just like that, Nick Bannister, the gay bully, was stalking away from my playground without a punch.

"Silly ass faggots," he murmured, under his breath as he left.

I locked the door behind him and went back to Rick who was sitting on the sofa with his head in his hands, showing me that the last of his secrets was out, the secret that he was indeed capable of losing it. I sat down next to him and he lay down, putting his head in my lap as I stroked his hair. He agitated quietly for a few minutes, I luckily having snatched a few Kleenexes out of the box on my way back. When he sat up, red eyed, he smiled at me.

"Sorry about that little outburst," he said. "I guess that was something that needed to happen sooner or later."

"I love you," I said softly, drying his cheeks with the Kleenex, "and I love you more now that I've seen this. Promise me that you're not going to hold anything back from me, whatever it is, that you can just let it all out? Promise me that there aren't going to be any secrets between us."

"Promise," he said, making the Girl Scout salute to go with it. "Just promise me you won't ever answer the fucking door ever again."

I gathered him up in my arms and turned on a *Golden Girls* DVD to lighten the mood. After three episodes, we were laughing again, Rick having expelled the things he needed to expel and me having proven that my fear about our relationship was silly.

When my cell phone rang, I was afraid to pick it up until I saw that it was Stephen calling from his cell. The rehab staff had taken it away from him when he went in.

"Guess what?" he said, in the immature voice that I knew so well. "I'm on my way to Atlanta with Nick."

"You're what?" I asked, not believing it at all, as if he could make a joke like that.

"Yep," he said, "I'm gonna sell the house and move in with Nick. He says hi, by the way."

The bastard did not even tell poor, misjudging Stephen what had happened that night.

"Good luck," I said absentmindedly, trying unsuccessfully to find the right words. "I hope it works out."

I did hope that it worked, but I just could not worry about it anymore because it was obvious that no sense had rubbed off on Stephen, that he was just as dependent as before.

"Stay in touch," I said before cutting the call.

After I explained this to Rick, we both agreed that it was good riddance. These problems would not be part of our problems. It was our turn now.

CHAPTER 27

▼

LOVE FOUND A HOME

We bought Stephen's house two weeks later, one of the most impulsive and uncalculated acts I had ever been a part of. The conversation came up one night while Rick and I were sitting on the sofa watching the late night news shows, something we did regularly together, but the discussion was always of a very different nature.

"I was thinking," he said, "about buying Stephen's house. It's in a great location, good size, but not really my taste on the decorating. It's got a pool and a high hedge all the way around. You know what that means?"

"The gardener has got to have a great ass because he has to climb up those big hedges in the backyard?" I asked, not really following him.

"Skinny dipping," he said as he sat up. "We can get naked in the pool and no one can see us."

"Us?"

"Of course, us. Who else would I be skinny dipping with? Maybe …"

I hesitated, knowing where he was going but not quite ready to admit that I was heading there, too.

"Maybe," he continued, "we should buy it together. This is our chance to have an awesome home … together."

For once I did not think about the risk. "Let's do it," I answered, quickly, with a confidence in my voice that, for once came from actually being confident.

"We can split the redecorating costs," Rick said, "or even use the equity, that is if we have equity, could you put any money down?"

Finally, a conversation about money did not make me nervous or agitated. I made the mental calculations in my head and came up with a figure that Rick matched, giving us a pretty good deal on buying Marilyn Clark's house.

"This is a big commitment," I said, as if neither one of us realized it.

"No shit," Rick said, laughing, "but we're not getting any younger. I say go for it when you've found the right thing. I survived you in casts and slings, bitching up a storm and just plain mean sometimes. I can live with it. That house has two separate master suites and a spare bedroom and bath. You could poop by yourself wherever you wanted to, baby."

"Can we buy new furniture?" I asked, excited like a child.

"Whatever you want," he replied seriously. "Whatever you want. This is it for me. If you don't want me, I'm done. I mean it. If this doesn't work out, I'm through with men. No more."

"Don't say that," I said, climbing into his lap to face him. "What if I died or something?"

"Widower," he said sharply. "We're both Southerners. I would be the Widower Monette for the rest of my life. I'd surround myself with young good-looking friends and be done with it. Maybe get a cat."

"What about these places?" I asked, sweeping my arm theatrically to indicate our current apartments.

"Let's rent them out," he answered, as if he had already thought it through. "This way, we keep the investment and the apartments, just in case."

The discussion did not last longer than that because my urge to kiss him took over. Any heavy kissing between us always led to the bedroom, or the floor, or the sofa, or the kitchen table. As our clothes started to pile up on the floor, I thought about the fact that I could make things right with the universe by having real sex with the man I loved in the Clark's house instead of disgustingly taking advantage of Stephen there. When we were getting ready to go to bed, I did have to bring up the obvious risk of buying a place together.

"What if …" I started, but did not finish, mesmerized by Rick's butt in his boxer briefs, his hand lightly scratching his left cheek in a manly way.

He was getting good at finishing my thoughts. "What if we split up?" he asked. "Well, Mr. Risk Management, we draw up a contract that says how we would proceed, probably selling to get back our original investments and to split whatever value had accumulated. We could also write in what happens in case one of us kicks the bucket. Our family attorney can whip that up pretty quickly."

"And how do we put our name on the mailbox?" I asked, with the sarcastic tone in my voice that Rick had come to love. "Is it Palini-Monette or Mon-ette-Palini? I insist on top billing!"

"Funny," he said, leaping over the bed to grab me again.

We decided that I should call Stephen the next day to tell him that we would buy the house. I was also hoping to get some idea of how things were really going in Atlanta, so I did my best to hint around. Stephen agreed immediately to our proposal to buy the house and insisted that he would call the real estate agent right away. He was actually very thankful, knowing that he was getting a good deal and plenty of cash up front, too. He wasn't very forthcoming when I asked him how it was shaping up with Nick.

"Fine," he lied, and even over the phone I could figure this one out. "The place is really cool, in Virginia Highlands, so we get to walk everywhere."

"And are you getting a job?" I asked.

"I have a few resumes out," he informed me, "but Nick told me I didn't need to worry about it right away. I've been doing a lot of cooking and shopping, so it's been good for me."

I decided that Nick's insistence on waiting for a job was his way of controlling Stephen, of making sure he could keep tabs on him. It made me angry to think about it and a little scared for Stephen. Rick and I had talked about the whole sit-uation a few days after Nick took Stephen with him, Rick insisting that I had done what I could and I insisting that I could do more. This was our first big dis-agreement, the fact that I was still trying to influence Stephen's choices even though he thought it was time to walk away. Rick and I agreed to disagree, hop-ing that the problem would keep itself in Atlanta, just far enough away to be in the background.

"Gotta go!" Stephen interrupted our small talk, "Nick will be home soon and I need to get something ready to eat."

It was hard for me to let it go, but I did. After the closing, Rick and I set about changing the house to suit our collective tastes, which were really not that far apart. The master suite we chose was not the one Mrs. Clark lived in, but the other one, and we had a great time turning it into a love nest for two. We started out intending to strip wallpaper and paint on our own, but it ended up being too much work and way too much of a distraction. One evening I went there after a long day and a long workout, and Rick was up on the ladder, priming one of the walls. He was wearing a bandana and cut-off jean shorts, with no shirt, the primer having spattered down on him a few times. I again couldn't resist him.

Once we were both covered with primer, we decided that we would hire one of the many over-the-top gay decorators we knew, complete with a retinue of twenty-something decorator-porn star wannabes to finish the job. When it was done, I insisted on giving the house a final scrub down to ensure its absolute cleanliness, to which Rick offered to hire a cleaning crew. I refused, wanting to make sure it was done my way the first time. The cleaning day was about a week before we moved in so Rick was outside doing yard work and I was inside scrubbing. As I made my way through the kitchen cabinets, which were really pretty spotless even though Stephen was a pig and his mother was not, I came across a small, leather-bound journal. It wasn't locked, so I opened it. Inside, the first half of the pages were written by Mrs. Clark and the second quarter was obviously in Stephen's handwriting. Mrs. Clark's entries described the way she felt when she found the lump and how her doctor insisted that it was early enough to do something about it. She wrote about her feelings about her ex-husband and expressed anger over his decision to leave her for the younger woman, although Mrs. Clark wrote that she did not blame the new Mrs. Clark and held no anger toward her. As I read on, expecting to feel guilty but actually feeling that I was somehow venerating Mrs. Clark, I found that she felt terrible grief over her sons, that she had tried her best to point them in the right direction and constantly questioned if it was her direction that caused them to go haywire. I got the picture that this was not going well, that the progression of these writings was leading to one final outcome.

On the last page of Mrs. Clark's writing, she poignantly described giving birth to both of them, but went into more detail about how she always felt a special bond with Stephen. She wondered if it was this bond that caused him to be gay and hoped that, regardless of what he was, he would find happiness someday.

"In the meantime," she wrote, "I hope Alex can take care of my wayward son, that he can provide some kind of guidance that I was somehow not able to give him. To my family, I do what I do because I have failed as a wife and as a mother. I have a beautiful home, a luxury car, and a closet full of designer clothing but that does not make you successful. Now I'm sick and I don't want the world to remember me as a sick woman who failed her family. Stephen, if you read this, understand that I love you and I am trusting you to keep the real reason for my death a secret somehow."

I sat down on the floor, not believing what I was reading, but drawn to continue. Stephen's writing was surprisingly coherent and intelligent, the first page pouring out his guilt at failing his mother, not her failing him.

"Mom," he wrote, "this wasn't your fault. You did what you could. I started down a path because I hated who I was. You didn't make me who I was, in fact, you made me into a real man, a sensitive man with feelings toward the world. Who I became, however, was completely different than what you made, and I did not blame you for that. I loved you, too, Mom."

I flipped a few pages, almost unable to continue, but again wondering how I had gotten hold of this book. One of the final pages threw me for a loop.

"Alex," Stephen wrote, as if he were going to send this to me, "I never loved you like you are supposed to love your better half. I realize now that I loved you because you are the one who tried to take over after my mother, the one who wanted to give me direction, help, and a shoulder to cry on, and I ignored you. You always tried. The night my mom died, I really didn't know how else to deal with it so that's why you had to take care of me. I was too afraid to ask you so I got myself fucked up. I'll have to tell you the story about my mother someday, but just not now. It's still too fresh in my mind to talk about. Don't give up on me, Alex. It's true that we could never be together, but you have really become like my older brother, the one I never had. You have a sense and a knowledge that I admire and I hope someday I can be like you. I don't know why I do the things I do, but I know that there is usually a point where I realize the mistake I am right in the middle of making. Thanks for being there for me. I love you."

The page looked as if it had been ripped about a quarter of the way down, as if Stephen was actually planning to rip it out and then stopped. I sat there, having read the final moments of a desperately unhappy woman and the response from her fairly sensible-sounding son. I really had done what I could. I hoped that, up until Stephen left with Nick, I had managed to help Stephen enough to honor Mrs. Clark's strange yet hopeful request the night of her planned death. If Stephen never called out for help again, at least he would have the help that I gave him in the past. I went on cleaning, certain that Mrs. Clark would have enjoyed what we did to the place and that she could rest easy knowing that her home would once again be a place where there was more love than anything else.

CHAPTER 28

▼

AN IMPERFECT ARRANGEMENT

Rick and I took a few days vacation to move in, making sure that everything went exactly where we wanted it. The pictures went on the walls the same day, the two of us finally stopping, exhausted, around two or three o'clock in the morning. For once we were too tired to make love, but we had already christened the house during the redecoration. Summer would change to fall soon so we also took advantage of having the pool, spending a couple of hours each morning frolicking naked in the water, swimming, and messing around like teenagers. Every night we wandered around in our house, talking about how unbelievable it was that this was *our* house and that we were *together*, really together. I knew Ayers would be happy for me because this is what we had planned together a few years before, a happy home where love held everything together.

We decided to have a "our people", which meant Stuart plus one and Madison and family, over for a cookout by the pool before the weather turned cool. The day of the party turned out hot, perfect for the pool so Rick and I decided to get our skinny dip in before everyone arrived. We were laying in the same chaise lounge, still naked, trying to remember that we would have guests showing up soon, when we heard Stuart's voice over the hedge.

"Get your clothes on, bitches!" he shouted. "You've got company!"

We threw on our cutest square-cut bathing suits and rushed to the front door, where Stuart waited impatiently with a much younger guy, who was tall and lean with a handsome face and big brown eyes. Stuart never hid his man-hungry nature, so he growled loudly when he looked at Rick and me in our bathing suits. I gave Stuart the eyes that said, "Please explain who this man is ..."

"Rick, Alex," he said, "This is Vaclav. He's from Romania."

"Czech Republic," interjected Vaclav in perfect English. "How do you do?"

He shook our hands like a perfect gentleman and allowed us to show him out to the back yard.

"He's much too mannered for you, honey," I whispered to Stuart.

"I know," answered Stuart. "But it works for now."

As it turned out, Vaclav had studied at the Sorbonne and returned to Prague to work before entering the Art Academy in Memphis to get his Ph.D. He looked twenty-one but was actually twenty-six, and when he got into his Speedo we all agreed that he could very well have been in one of those foreign porno films that we all liked so much. Madison arrived a few minutes later, along with Peter and the boys, who ran quickly out to the pool, where Rick had been sure to have pool toys for them to play with.

"Love what you've done to the place," she said.

I sat down at the table in the kitchen, looking out at my back yard. Madison was laying on the side of the pool, still svelte in her bikini, hair up, holding a pina colada, looking very much like an old Hollywood starlet in big white sunglasses. Peter, equally as sexy at forty, was towing the two boys around on a raft, laughing as they tried to splash their starlet of a mom. Rick was flipping burgers over the grill, his cute cotton shirt open, revealing that awesome tan body, yelling to each person about the specific doneness of his or her burger. Stuart was rubbing lotion on Vaclav, who looked as if he could easily end up with a sunburn, while talking loudly about who makes the decision as to what is art and what is not. Was this my perfect arrangement?

As always a knock on the door interrupted the perfection of the moment, but I thought it was Jen, who had promised to stop by. No one heard the doorbell so I went alone, planning to ask Jen and her boyfriend to stay for a burger and a pina colada. The entryway of our new house was such a stark contrast to the back door of my much smaller apartment. It was really a marble foyer, with a ceiling that went up about twelve feet, with a huge front door that opened out onto a smaller, garden style courtyard with a wrought iron gate and the doorbell. There was no peeking out curtains, so I cracked open the big door to look out into the courtyard and was shocked to see Stephen standing there, his duffle bag slung over his shoulder, his opposite wrist wrapped in a brace.

Good God, I thought as I went out into the courtyard. "What the hell?" I said out loud, not really to anyone, but Stephen answered.

"Hi," he said. "Bet you're surprised to see me here, huh?"

"Um, yes," I said, still watching him from the other side of the gate. "What happened?"

"Maybe you could let me in first," he said, eyeing the gate.

I immediately had a flashback to the journal I had read, sitting on the floor before we moved in, reading with disbelief as I found out the truth about his mother and then about him. I wasn't sure if I could ever bring it up, but I knew that Stephen came here because he needed someone. I let him in and we went into the front parlor, right near the closet where the drag queen discovered Rick and I making out.

"Well, it didn't quite work out," he said. "There were some problems. Nick kept doing drugs and I tried my best to resist. Of course, when I demanded that he stop, that it wasn't fair, we fought. That's how this happened."

He held up his wrist, but I suspected there had probably been a lot more damage than that.

"So, last week he went out and I stayed home," Stephen continued, "and I got a call from one of his friends at about four in the morning ..."

My eyes widened, the fear of what happened next showed immediately on my face. Stephen read this right away.

"Nick's dead," he said, no emotion, just a fact. "It was too much, and he overdosed. They said he went into cardiac arrest. They got him to a hospital but it happened again and that did it."

Again I was shocked, a lump rising in my throat, not wanting to believe it even though Nick was not anyone I would have cared to be around again.

"Do you think I could stay here for a few days?" he asked. "I have a job interview at FedEx in the accounting department, so as soon as I have an idea I'll find a place."

"You're way too calm," I accused him. "Are you on something? I mean, are you in shock about Nick or something?"

"I'm not on anything," he said indignantly, "and I wasn't really shocked about Nick. I'm not sure why I did that, because I didn't love him. The sex was great, but he was just an asshole. I'm not sorry he's gone."

"We've got to get Rick and explain it to him," I said. "You picked a hell of a day to come back here with this. We've got company."

"Sorry," he said. "I always seem to do a good job of fucking things up for you."

"Nothing can fuck this up," I said with a smile.

"Alex?" Stephen asked, a bit of humility creeping into his voice. "Did you find the journal?"

"I did," I replied, patting his shoulder. "And I understand. We won't say anything about it. You were hoping I'd find it, weren't you?"

Stephen didn't reply. He just smiled that winning smile.

The scene outside was the same, so I motioned for Rick to come inside. Peter jumped out of the pool and took over the barbeque, a move that could not have been better if it had been rehearsed. I stopped Rick in the doorway.

"Stephen's back," I said, waiting for his reaction.

"No surprise there," he said, obviously unmoved.

"There's more," I said as Stephen stepped into the kitchen and took a seat at the table. "You should sit."

Rick sat down without a word to Stephen, but put his hand lightly on his shoulder as he did.

"It's Nick," I said, looking straight at Rick, with my hand over his. "He overdosed. He didn't make it."

Rick made a slight grimace with his face, closing his eyes briefly and tightening his grip on my hand. I could see that the small part of Rick that once had feelings for his ex was reacting, trying to find reason in something that seemed senseless. He turned to Stephen.

"Were you with him?" he asked.

"No," Stephen said quietly.

"Was he alone?" Rick asked.

"No," Stephen said, again quietly, with just a slight touch of pain on his face.

Nick, in one of his fits of anger, had gone out with some friends, insisting that Stephen stay home and keep out of his business. Nick had been doing a few lines of coke, Stephen explained, which always made him agitated and jumpy, but that night it seemed to be excessive. He went to a bar with a group of friends and then headed off to a sex party, where crystal meth was the stimulus of choice and where anything was acceptable. No one noticed that Nick had slipped off with a couple of guys, and when one of the guys came back to them, white faced and freaked out, Nick had already gone into cardiac arrest. He was not quite stable when he made it to the hospital, and as they debated whether to call Stephen or not, the doctor came out to tell them that he just could not save Nick. His friends called Stephen, who reacted calmly and with a guilty relief. Stephen told them to call Nick's family, gathered his things, and checked into a hotel. Hopefully this would be the last bad choice he would make.

"Did his family take care of things?" Rick asked.

"Yes," Stephen replied. "I left so that they could deal with it."

"Goddammit," said Rick, pounding his fist on the table. "Stupid, stupid, stupid."

Stephen and I didn't have a reaction to this, so we sat in silence for a minute.

"Just give me a few minutes?" Rick asked, and then turned to Stephen. "You look like hell. Have you eaten? Have a burger."

I took Stephen outside where Madison and Stuart looked shocked to see him. I simply announced that Stephen would be staying for a few days until he could find a place. I took them aside to tell them what had happened to Nick, which again was not a shock. After a few minutes, Rick appeared with one of our two woks, the oldest one, which was probably on its way to the dump. He held a large manila envelope in the other hand and had a big smile on his face. He took his glass, clinked it with a fork, and instructed everyone to gather around the table. From the manila envelope, he produced some pages of stationery he had never really used, along with a few pens.

"We're saying goodbye to the past today," he announced, "so everyone take a piece of paper and a pen. Write something there, write down what you are saying goodbye to, write a book or write one word. You don't have to tell us what it is. Go on now, everyone."

For a split second, I thought that he had lost his mind, but then I realized that he was helping us all deal with some sort of grief. Everyone seemed to like the idea, even Vaclav, who was totally new to the group and could have been scared away very easily. Even Madison's kids were eagerly writing on their pages, helped along by their Mom and Dad. I wrote a farewell of sorts to Ayers, an affirmation that it was time for me to embrace love again, to finish up the fantasy that he and I had dreamed up. I knew he would understand and felt closer to his memory at that moment than ever before. Rick placed his envelope in the wok, which I later learned contained a photo of Nick and a written description of one of the bad fights they had.

"My past," he said, "is going bye-bye. I have started over with the most wonderful guy in the world, my first love."

I struggled for a moment and then realized that Rick had just admitted to our friends that I was his first love. I saw that this man knew what he wanted for almost forty years and did not settle for less until he was convinced he found it. I had sort of wandered into this by accident, although at that moment I began to question whether accidents were really accidental. All of my doubts melted away as the words "my first love" echoed in my head. All of my wondering about how many chances we got was answered easily. You get as many chances as it takes to figure it out. Rick and I had figured it out, and I knew that there was nothing left to worry about. Stuart stepped up next, folding his paper in half and placing it gently in the middle of the wok.

"Undisclosed hangup," he said, winking at me.

Madison's oldest, Benjamin, said ceremoniously, "I'm not gonna be scared of math anymore," and dropped his paper in the wok.

The youngest, Matthew, said in that voice that only a child could have, "Bye to Missus Fitzgerald, cuz she's a mean old lady."

Madison dropped her paper in, adding softly, "Also an undisclosed hangup. Bye bye!"

Peter slipped his page in between his wife and kids, saying only, "A past grudge."

Madison smiled lightly with her eyes closed when she heard this.

Vaclav and Stephen put their pages together without saying anything. Then I did the same, thinking that further talk would not be appropriate.

"Stand back!" shouted Rick, pulling out the long handled matches he bought specifically for the fireplace and the planned sexual encounters on the rug in front of it. He struck a match, placed it under the pile of paper, and held it there for a second. Within a few more seconds, the whole pile was on fire and everyone stood around the table looking up at the smoke that went up from it. We let it burn until a pile of crispy ashes was left, when Rick picked it up with much pomp and marched it over to the barbeque grill, where he dumped the ashes onto the charcoal.

"Who's for another burger?" he shouted, and suddenly the life was back in the party, actually a life that had never been there suddenly appeared, as all of us had entered the backyard attached to certain things that kept us down and now we were without those things. I stood behind Rick, putting my arms around his waist, holding him tight, as the kids' laughter filled the air.

We held our commitment ceremony on Christmas Eve, in the foyer of our house, surrounded by decorations that would have been over the top in anyone else's home, but not ours. We decided on Christmas Eve because it was our favorite holiday as kids, the magic of Christmas something we had tried so hard to recapture over the years without success. That night, candles glowed in every part of the house and the Christmas tree shined with its thousands of lights. Rick and I, along with our guests, were dressed in suits and evening gowns, the sequins shimmering from the light of the tree and the candles. The sight of all of this brought the magic back and added to it. As the preacher from our local church read the ceremony of commitment, I looked around the foyer slowly, trying to capture every expression, every person. Of course Rick was the hottest person there; his black suit form-fitted over his physique, those green eyes sparkling brighter than any Christmas tree.

In six months of living together, we fit together perfectly, each one the compliment of the other, our home full of love and peace, the two things we had both been trying to find for so long. I was no longer worried and no longer angry at the world for taking Ayers away. It was what it was, and Ayers' voice would always be a part of me, his snapping fingers would always stay in my mind, and his love would take me from one place in my life to the next. Rick seemed to become happier each day, even on the bad days, his spirits visibly lifting the second he set foot in the house, holding me tight and asking me to tell him about my day. The act of moving on had been painful, but that Christmas Eve the pain was worthwhile.

Madison and Peter, the handsome couple, stood proudly on the fringe, their second honeymoon obviously in full swing. Stuart, dressed in a velvet smoking jacket and ascot, holding his fifth glass of champagne, stood beside them, smiling his real smile, the smile of someone who had somehow figured out how to be happy. Even my parents and the Monettes turned up for the event, not sure they understood what we were doing but wanting to see our happiness. Stephen stood with Vaclav, his arm around Vaclav's waist, the two having become an item a few weeks after the day by the pool. Vaclav approached me during the pool party, and although my better judgment told me to put him off of Stephen, I told him I would say something, just like an old world matchmaker. Their first date was a transformation, the immature Stephen walking away for good and the mature Stephen taking his place with the one we all hoped was the right person. I thought about Stephen and knew that he viewed Rick and I as his pseudo-parents, big brothers who were always around to give advice or help him out of a tough spot. Stephen had rented my apartment a few days after he showed up at the pool party, then immediately secured the accounting job. I explained that I would kick him out if he didn't pay the rent, and so far, he was early each month. That night they asked my permission to allow Vaclav to move in without raising the rent, to which I replied with a snap of my fingers, "You go, boy!"

The group around us was possibly not the group we would have chosen, but they were the group that ended up with us. We wished we had parents who automatically got what being gay was all about, but we didn't. We wished that we didn't have to worry about what could possibly be Stephen's next drama, but we did because he trusted us and we wanted to see him succeed. We wished that we didn't have to live from day to day hoping that medicine found a cure for what could possibly take Rick away from me, but we did. As I looked around that night, I realized that I had found it, the place where I always needed to be, the place where the same issues faced us but formed a circle around Rick and I, the two of us waiting to fight off anything that came our way, that place that I had once called a perfect arrangement, now an imperfect arrangement with Rick and I as the center of it. The perfect arrangements, Rick once told me, only looked perfect from the outside. Our imperfect arrangement was happily flawed yet real, and looking around at our group and back into Rick's eyes that magical Christmas Eve, I knew I could live with that.